D0736100

The Wereling

BY
STEPHEN COLE

Book Two

PREY

razOr
bill
NEW YORK

The Wereling: Prey

RAZORBILL

Published by the Penguin Group
Penguin Young Readers Group
345 Hudson Street, New York, New York 10014, U.S.A.
Penguin Group (USA) Inc., 375 Hudson Street, New York,
New York 10014, U.S.A.
Penguin Books Canada Ltd, 10 Alcorn Avenue, Toronto,
Ontario, Canada M4V 3B2 (a division of Pearson Penguin Canada, Inc.)
Penguin Books Ltd, 80 Strand, London WC2R 0RL, England
Penguin Ireland, 25 St Stephen's Green, Dublin 2, Ireland
(a division of Penguin Books Ltd)
Penguin Group (Australia), 250 Camberwell Road, Camberwell,
Victoria 3124, Australia (a division of Pearson Australia Group Pty Ltd)
Penguin Books India Pvt Ltd, 11 Community Centre, Panchsheel Park,
New Delhi – 110 017, India
Penguin Group (NZ), Cnr Airborne and Rosedale Roads, Albany,
Auckland 1310, New Zealand (a division of Pearson New Zealand Ltd)
Penguin Books (South Africa) (Pty) Ltd, 24 Sturdee Avenue,
Rosebank, Johannesburg 2196, South Africa

Penguin Books Ltd, Registered Offices: 80 Strand,
London WC2R 0RL, England

10 9 8 7 6 5 4 3 2 1

Copyright © Working Partners Ltd 2004
All rights reserved

Originally published in the United Kingdom by Bloomsbury Publishing Plc,
38 Soho Square, London, W1D 3HB

Library of Congress Cataloging-in-Publication Data

Cole, Stephen, 1971-
  Prey / by Stephen Cole.
    p. cm. — (The wereling ; book 2)
  Summary: Kate and Tom flee to New York City as they continue to seek a cure
for Tom's half-human/half-werewolf state, finding old enemies and new friends
there while eluding the police, who believe them to be murderers.
  ISBN 1-59514-042-5 (pbk.)
  [1. Werewolves—Fiction. 2. Fugitives from justice—Fiction. 3. Gangs—
Fiction. 4. New York (N.Y.)—Fiction. 5. Horror stories.] I. Title. II. Series:
Cole, Stephen, 1971- Wereling ; bk. 2.
  PZ7.C67356Pr 2005
  [Fic]—dc22
                                                                    2004026071

Printed in the United States of America

To Jill

CHAPTER ONE

The full moon shone in on Tom Anderson through the truck window. It felt like a searchlight, hunting him down. He shifted his weight on the backseat, squirming clear of the blazing light while still pretending to be asleep.

He hated hitching rides, especially at night. The moonlight put him on edge, made him feel shivery and sweaty and caged in. Feigning sleep spared him the ordeal of making conversation with the over-curious truck driver.

Not that he was exactly the focus of attention, with Kate up front in the passenger seat. There was no doubt in Tom's mind that it was Kate who had brought the truck screeching to a halt on the highway out of Philadelphia. Tall and slim and dressed all in black, her long dark hair whipped around by the cold October gusts, she was like a secret weapon in the world of thumbing lifts.

Good thing. They needed to get to New York fast.

Opening his eyes a fraction, Tom snuck a look out of the window. Beyond the skeletons of loading platforms and stacks of empty truck containers that lined the turnpike, he saw about a billion pinpricks of light stacked in long, tall grids against the night. They were nearing the city—but maybe not fast enough, Tom decided, as the big, bearded driver stole another lingering glance at Kate.

"So, how come a sweet thing like you is hitching, anyway?"

"Well . . ." Kate shrugged. "Hitching's cheap . . . and I guess me and Tom just enjoy the freedom."

Freedom, Tom thought bitterly. Sure: freedom to creep and crawl through this horrible new life that had been thrust on him. Freedom to live in fear, constantly looking back over his shoulder. Waking and wondering if today was the day their pursuers would catch up with them at last.

They had to keep moving, to keep one step ahead. But since they didn't have the cash for a bus ticket past Philly, Kate—practical as ever—had dolled herself up and they'd hit the highway. He knew she hated to hitch, loathed the way the long-distance drivers looked her over, like wolves salivating over their next meal.

Nice analogy.

Tom shifted irritably in the seat once more.

"You kids are pretty young to be on the road, ain't you? How old are you, sugar?"

"We're both eighteen," Kate answered. "Taking a year off before college."

Life on the run has made you a pretty good liar, Kate, Tom decided. Kate was actually seventeen, Tom a year younger. He'd been looking forward to his eighteenth birthday pretty much all his life. He'd always imagined it would be the day he'd walk out the front door and suddenly find himself a man, ready to make his mark in the world.

That was before he'd got tangled up with Kate and her family and found his future screwed to hell.

Found himself a werewolf.

"So . . ." There was a pause. "Is Tom your boyfriend?"

"Not really," Kate said, turning her head away to look through the window. "No."

Tom indulged himself in a bitter half smile. How could Kate ever begin to think of him as boyfriend material, knowing what he had become? Knowing that if they ever *did* get together . . .

He imagined the look on the trucker's face if Kate told him the whole story: that her family were werewolves, creatures believed lost to legend but in reality part of an active and totally secret subculture whose population stretched clear around the world. That as a pureblood female her latent lupine nature would be woken if she mated with another 'wolf. And that Tom had been kidnapped by Kate's family and held prisoner in their house while they turned him into

3

future son-in-law material—turned him 'wolf too.

The plan hadn't worked. Kate didn't *want* to embrace her lupine heritage. She was determined to stay human. So she and Tom had escaped. But in doing so, they'd made many enemies in the lupine community—including Kate's mother, Marcie Folan.

The real joke, Tom reflected, was that with all they'd been through trying to stay alive, he had never felt closer to anyone than Kate.

"So you and Sleeping Beauty in the back there, you're just good friends, right?"

"Right," Kate replied, a hard, tired edge creeping into her voice. "But Tom is pretty special, you know?"

Special. Uh-huh, Tom thought wryly.

He was what the lupine community termed a silverblood—someone with exceptional resistance to the 'wolf change. They'd turned him in the end, but he'd come out of the whole process a wereling. *"Very rare,"* Kate had informed him, quoting some ancient, secret text: *"A wereling is a resister whose humanity and compassion prevail in the 'wolf."* Which seemed to mean that when the change was on him, Tom could hold on to some struggling, screaming human part of his nature that loathed what he had become.

But each time Tom changed into the lupine state, he wondered if this would be the time he would lose control and give in to the intoxicating power of being 'wolf.

They emerged from a tunnel, and the sky was suddenly neon bright under the orange-pink glare of streetlights. The truck swerved and took an exit. They were heading north, Tom noted.

"So this is Manhattan," Kate observed. Her habitual deadpan voice made it hard to know if she was impressed or just plain bored.

"Sure is," agreed their driver. "What a sight, huh? Day or night."

Tom had to agree. On their left was the wide dark stretch of the Hudson River, and on the right, buildings so high the moon barely peeked over them. As they wove through a crisscross of streets and avenues, Tom felt a sense of genuine awe. It was like he was traveling through a canyon of metal and glass, dwarfed by the gargantuan size of the skyscrapers all around him.

Their driver turned a corner and gave a huge pantomime yawn. "Say, it's almost two already. Need a place to stay tonight?"

"No thanks."

"Hey, come on. I got a comfortable place, sweetheart. There's even room for your friend."

Kate's voice hardened. "I said, *no thanks*."

"How about a little gratitude, huh?" The trucker's voice got throatier. "I've brought you all this way. Seems like you owe me something in return."

Tom clenched his fists. He'd been tense before, but now he could feel his heart beat harder with anger. He was about to speak out when he caught sight of Kate in the rearview mirror, subtly shaking her head at him. "Not here," she mouthed.

"Would you let us out now, please?" she asked the driver.

"Why break up the party?" The big guy pressed a fleshy hand down on Kate's thigh.

"Let go of her," Tom snarled, grabbing hold of the man's thick arm.

"Yeah?" The trucker took a right turn and broke Tom's grip easily as he did so. "What are you going to do about it, squirt?"

"He'll turn you into dog meat," Kate snapped, "unless you stop this truck and let us out right now."

"Him?" The big man tossed an amused glance back at Tom. "Don't you want a *real* man, honey?"

Tom leaned forward and growled at the driver. "You don't want to know how real I am."

Kate was winding down the window. "Unless you want me to scream loud enough to wake all Manhattan, you'll pull over right now."

The driver cursed under his breath and swung his rig to the side of the broad avenue. "Who needs this? Go on, get out of here, both of you."

Tom grabbed their stuff and got out. Kate followed him without a backward glance at the red-faced driver. With a last impotent blare on his horn, the man dodged back into the ragged traffic pushing down the avenue.

"Are you okay?" Tom asked her as they crossed to the sidewalk.

"Of course I'm okay," she said crossly. "You shouldn't have interfered. I can handle jerks like him."

"Sorry," Tom said, a little stung.

Kate sighed. "It's the full moon," she reminded him, more gently. "The more stressed out you get, the more you lose control, the easier it is for the 'wolf to get a hold on you."

Tom looked down at his boots, feeling the prickle on the back of his neck from the moonlight. He knew she was right. "So what do we do now?"

Kate had already taken her guidebook out of her backpack. "I guess we look for the nearest hostel."

"Can we afford one?"

"Not really. But at this hour I'd sooner find somewhere safe to crash for the night."

Tom sighed. "Too bad Blood's not here to lend us an apartment. A little luxury would be nice right now." They'd made one good friend during their crazy time in New Orleans—Adam Blood, a high-class realtor and head of a small network that kept tabs on the dark side of the city. They both owed him their lives. But when he'd taken a stand against Marcie Folan, Blood had gained a formidable enemy. His life had been in great danger, so he'd gone into hiding.

"I wonder where he is now?" Kate murmured.

"Living it up in the sun somewhere." Tom forced

a smile. "Lucky bastard." Shivering a little, he pulled up the collar of his denim jacket and walked to the corner to find a street sign. "West 107th Street and Manhattan Avenue," he called to Kate.

She nodded and unfolded the map at the back of the book.

Tom shoved both hands deep in his pockets and pushed out a deep breath. The moon had placed an itch under his skin, like ants were crawling inside him. Thank God for the tall buildings, which blocked him from its full effect. He paced up and down, avoiding the eyes of people drifting along the street. Any one of them could be a 'wolf, out looking for them. The lupine community was tight-knit despite the distance it spanned, and once the word was out against you, you weren't safe anywhere. "Do you realize how many people there must be in Manhattan alone, never mind the boroughs?"

Kate knew what he was getting at and swiftly rolled out her stock answer: "If Jicaque's here, we'll find him."

Jicaque—pronounced "Zhi-cah-key"—was the fabled medicine man with the tongue-twister name who might—*might*—be able to reverse Tom's lupine condition. According to Kate's research, Jicaque seemed to be the only chance they had. Unfortunately he was also about as easy to find as smoke in fog.

"Too bad your online contact couldn't be a little

more precise as to where Jicaque's staying," Tom remarked.

"He's working on that," Kate replied.

"Is he? Anyone could've sent that e-mail." Tom smoothed a clammy hand through his short dark hair, cold sweat spiking it up. "We've been tricked that way before. The 'wolves could've hacked into his account. Or hacked into *him,* forced him to spill those passwords you agreed—"

"You know, Tom, you're right," Kate said wearily. This was an old argument. "We *don't* know we can trust the guy who gave me the info; he's just a name in a chat room. And say we *do* manage to find Jicaque—we don't know that we can trust *him* either. But since it's the only lead we've got . . ."

Tom threw up his hands. "Yeah, yeah. You're right, I know." His insides felt cramped and jumpy. "I'm sorry."

"That's got to be the lamest apology I ever heard." Kate gave him a faint smile, then nodded toward the moon. "But I guess it *is* your time of the month, huh?"

Tom shot her a look. "You don't want to make jokes like that when I'm feeling like this." But Kate was grinning at him, and he found himself smiling back.

"We're right by Central Park," she said after a moment. She pointed down the block at a dark mass of trees behind a low stone wall. "We could camp out there for the night."

"Just you, me, and fifty muggers. Nice idea."

Kate shrugged. "We could bed down in some bushes. It's only a few hours till dawn. Then we can get up and start the search."

"If we haven't frozen to death first," grumbled Tom.

"Well, let's hear your great idea."

Tom swallowed hard. "I guess if we lie close together, it might not be so cold."

Kate's green eyes were cool and inquiring as she looked him over. "Tom Anderson, is that some kind of come-on?"

"Get over yourself!" Tom protested, and turned away so she wouldn't see him blush.

It was weird to see the dark, hunching shadows of so many trees suddenly rise from the center of the city. The park was quiet and gloomy as they crossed its borders and headed inside.

The wind had dropped, and the landscape held itself as still as the moon. As they pressed on, Tom's senses kicked into overdrive. He drank in the sweet scent of damp earth and dewy grass. Upwind, a loaded trash can was brimming over with bad smells.

Farther up the path they were taking, he heard a twig snap and caught a tang of sweat and desperation. Tom could almost picture the figure: some junkie, turned animal by his need for a fix, shivering in the foliage and psyching himself up to strike should someone pass by.

The moon seemed to shine brighter, and as its light needled Tom with greater strength, he felt a moment's kinship with the junkie. The animal inside him was desperate for release, to strike out and taste blood, to bring on the change.

"Tom?" Kate was looking at him, concerned.

"Not this way," he whispered.

They changed direction. For several minutes they pressed on quietly, searching for somewhere to bed down.

"How about here?" Kate suggested, gesturing to a small huddle of trees and bushes.

But as she started to explore, cracking and rustling through the foliage, Tom hushed her. He could hear footfalls on the wet grass, distant shouts, and ragged breaths getting closer. "People are coming," he hissed.

Kate looked around, but it was too dark to make out anything clearly. "Should we get out of here?" she asked.

Tom peered more deeply into the gloom. Across the open parkland he could see a kid no older than himself, who seemed to be running for his life. A gang of about ten people was tearing along after him, jeering and calling. Tom could smell the fear on the boy, felt his own heart start to pound faster, matching the rhythm of the kid's footfalls.

"Tom?" Kate tugged on his sleeve.

"They're chasing him down. Like it's a hunt or something." He turned to her, the hairs on the back of his neck prickling, his breath coming fast and shallow as though it were him running.

Kate shook her head. "Leave it, Tom. It's not our fight."

"I—I can scare them off," he said, staggering like a drunk, his voice slurring as the change crept closer. "Just scare them, that's all . . ."

"Tom?" Kate grabbed hold of his sweaty face with both hands, tried to make him look into her eyes. "Tom, no. Don't do this."

But a familiar heat was coursing through Tom's body. No turning back now. He saw the urgency in Kate's eyes turn to resignation. Then she moved forward to yank his jacket off. He fell to his knees, fumbling feverishly with the buttons on his cotton shirt. Too late. His torso was already swelling up, and the heavy fabric split at the seams.

He hunched forward on all fours, a sound raking out of his throat that was half choking and half laughter as he went into spasm. Tom's bones were melting under his skin, remolding themselves into lupine shape. Coarse dark hair pushed out of every pore. He felt a tickle in his gums as his teeth sprouted like spikes and his jaw pushed out. His spine twisted and lengthened, pelvis cracking like a gunshot as it clicked into a fresh position, hind legs twitching as new and powerful muscles fixed themselves there.

Tom reached back his head and bit and snapped at the tattered remains of his jeans. They fell away like the last vestiges of his human form. The moon warmed his bare back like a tropical sun. He began to run, luxuriating in the sweet strength of his sleek lupine body. His heavy paws tore up the ground, his blood roaring in his ears. Dimly, somewhere behind him, he caught Kate's scent, heard her running after him weighed down with their stuff.

Tom burst out from the cover of the trees just ahead of them all and roared.

Startled, the boy skidded on the wet grass and fell. He swore, his face twisted with pain as he clutched at his ankle. His shadowy pursuers also came slithering to a halt, panting for breath.

Tom leapt over the boy and bared his teeth at them.

They stared at the monster before them. But they didn't run screaming. Didn't even flinch. Instead their breathing grew deeper, hoarser. Their eyes began to shine with a sickly yellow light. One by one, they stretched up their arms and then bent forward onto all fours as their bodies began to change.

"Jesus," Tom heard Kate whisper. "They're 'wolves too."

CHAPTER TWO

Kate felt her insides twist. When the change came over Tom, he became a powerful, lithe, deep-chested creature, far larger than a real wolf. Tom's lupine form, with its dark, lustrous coat and muscular frame, was beautiful in its own way.

But there was no beauty or grace in the monsters that were now facing him. Wiry and rangy like the humans they had been, their fur was mottled and patchy, their teeth as yellow as their eyes, backs humped and misshapen. Two or three of them howled, a chilling sound like babies screaming. The rest, snapping their jaws, padded back and forth or in circles, as if easing themselves into their lupine movement.

Tom turned and glanced back at Kate. His eyes were still dark, still his own—the pale glow of the lupine shone there at the start of the change but soon dwindled and died. That set him apart from all other lupines Kate had ever seen, and she thanked God for this, his wereling strength. It helped her remember that Tom was still Tom, whatever form he was forced to take.

Suddenly Tom threw himself into the pack of awakening 'wolves.

"Tom, no!" Kate screamed.

The noise was dreadful. Barks and growls full of torment and anger echoed out into the starry night. But Kate saw that Tom was running rings around the creatures; he wasn't attacking them so much as goading them, taking their attention. Distracting them, she realized, so that she might help the boy and get them both the hell out of there.

She broke cover and ran over to their quarry, who was still down on the ground, slowly edging away from the angry pack. He was pretty for a boy, but his delicate features had been spoiled by a long scar that ran down his left cheek. He was olive skinned, Spanish maybe, with shaved hair.

When he saw her coming, he scrambled up painfully and held out his fists in warning. *"No te quiero hacer daño,"* he said warningly, his voice heavy and scared, "so get the hell away from me, bitch."

Kate groped around her ninth-grade Spanish for the translation, holding up her hands open palmed to reassure him. "I don't want to hurt you either," she said at last.

"You won't get the chance," he snarled. He turned and tried to run, but his injured ankle gave way under him and he crashed back down to the ground, swearing.

Kate was about to go after him when she caught sight of Tom. He'd broken clear of the pack and was trying to lead them away. Out for blood, the other lupines went bounding after him, their sinister shapes soon lost to the night.

Ten against one. They could tear Tom to ribbons.

Worried, Kate grabbed her bag and Tom's stuff and crossed to where the kid lay cursing and struggling on the ground. "What did you do?" she demanded.

"Damn ankle. It's sprained or something."

"I mean, what did you do to get a pack of werewolves chasing after you?"

He sneered at her. "And why are you on my case?"

"Because my friend just risked his life trying to save you," Kate responded fiercely. "You better be worth the rescue."

He snorted. "Rescue? I know what kind of rescue you got in mind, wolf girl." He mimed slitting his throat.

"I'm not one of them," she told him. "They're chasing after me like they are after you."

"So why do you hang out with wolf boy?"

"Tom's not like that scum chasing after you. Did you see his eyes?"

"I guess," the boy conceded. "Didn't look like howler eyes. Looked . . . normal."

"Tom is anything but normal. That's why the 'wolves are chasing after us too." Kate glanced about. "Come on. We'd better hide till it's safe."

She helped him scramble behind some prickly bushes, then they held themselves as still as possible, straining to hear any sound of the 'wolves coming back.

"I'm Kate," she breathed.

"Ramon," the boy replied. "Why are the howlers chasing you?"

"You ever hear of a guy called Takapa?"

Ramon stared at her. "If you messed with Takapa, I don't want nothing to do with you. He's the one screwing up this place. There's no howler bigger than him."

"That big *howler* is actually just a scrawny freak with good PR," Kate told him lightly, but she couldn't repress a shudder. Takapa was making a name for himself among the lupine community as some kind of freedom fighter. He believed that the 'wolves should come crawling out of the shadows to hunt and kill freely in the human world—and was working on ways to make it happen.

Ramon pointed a finger over her shoulder. "Look who's back."

Heart lurching, Kate twisted around.

It was Tom, human again, his pale skin laced silver

in the moonlight. He'd reclaimed the tatters of his jeans and was leaning heavily against a tree, soaking wet and shivering.

Kate quickly pulled out the last of his fresh clothes from his backpack. "Are you okay? What happened?"

"There's water back there, a reservoir or something," Tom said, gesturing behind him. "I took a swim. They lost my scent and went off the wrong way." He gratefully pulled on a sweater. "Lucky for us they're slow and stupid."

Tom nodded at Ramon, and Kate made some hurried introductions.

"We should get out of here." Tom eased his arms through the straps on his backpack. "Ramon, do you know a safe place we can stay tonight?"

Ramon shook his head. "No way, 'wolf. You're mixed up with Takapa."

"This *'wolf* just saved your life," Kate said. As she spoke, she could hear far-off sirens drawing closer.

Ramon winced like they were going off in his ear. He tried to stand and gasped with pain."

"Okay," he said, scowling. "You can hide out at my place tonight. But then you're gone."

"Very generous of you," Tom observed wryly.

Together they helped Ramon up. His clothes reeked of sweat and cigarette smoke, and Kate nearly gagged. But after a few stumbling steps they managed to fall into a kind of limping gait that allowed them to move at a pretty fast pace.

"I hope the police don't find those 'wolves—for *their* sake," Kate muttered.

"They won't." Ramon shook his head. "The wolves ain't as stupid as you think. They stick to the shadows so no one knows the truth."

Tom shot him a sideways glance. "And the truth is?"

"That they're recruiting," Ramon said simply. "Cops don't know they're there. . . . The nice people of the city don't know they're there. . . . But in the bad neighborhoods, the places that my people live in, those bastards are getting stronger all the time."

Ramon's hangout was in a tenement on 110th Street. It was a hell of a walk, but somehow they made it. Tom and Kate helped Ramon up the steps.

He knocked on the pitted, battered old door in a distinctive tattoo. "You better keep quiet about being a howler," he warned Tom.

"Sure. Believe it or not," Tom replied, "it's not something I like to advertise."

A minute or so later some bolts were thrown and the door creaked open a little.

A Polaroid camera pushed its way out and Tom was blinded by its flash.

"Quit that, Polar," Ramon complained, and shoved open the door.

Polar backed up and shrugged. He was a tall

skinny kid with skin the same color as Ramon's, but beyond that Tom couldn't really say, since Polar kept the camera up to his face. He plucked out the developing picture and silently handed it to Kate.

She stared at it, baffled, then slipped it in her purse.

"Life looks better to Polar through his camera," was all Ramon offered by way of explanation.

They were standing in a filthy, dusty kitchen. Damp mold had crawled up around the black-painted windows, and there seemed to be more plaster on the garbage-strewn floor than on the walls.

The look of disdain was clear on Kate's face.

"Hey, this is just the lobby," Ramon assured her, and pointed in the direction Polar was disappearing. "Presidential suite's through there."

"Ramon? You back? *Tienes algún problema?*" A girl's voice, hard and clear in its urgency, carried through to them.

"No, es nada," he called back. At once he shook off the support of Tom and Kate and stood up alone.

Tom understood why when a second later, a girl with a nose stud swept into the scuzzy room. She wore a red cropped top beneath a hooded sweat-shirt, and tight black pants. Her thick black hair had been pulled back away from her high forehead. Hands on her hips, her wide, appraising eyes full of attitude, Tom imagined she took some impressing.

20

"This is Jasmine," Ramon told Tom with a crooked smile. "She loves me."

The girl held up her middle finger to him. "Bite me," she said. Her disparaging gaze moved to Tom and then lingered on Kate. "Who you got here?"

"Kate and Tom. They're okay. Helped me out."

Jasmine arched one finely plucked eyebrow. "Why didn't you call me?"

"Lost my cell somewhere in the park," Ramon replied.

"We heard on the radio something was happening in Central Park," Jasmine went on. "Tony's gang?"

Ramon nodded. "Turned hairy on me. No chance of us teaming up with Tony's crew—they're howlers, all of them."

Kate was looking at Jasmine in disbelief. "They broadcast about the 'wolves on the radio?"

"Sure," said Jasmine, her pretty face twisting into a sneer. "It went out on Hot 97."

"We got a police radio out back, 28th Precinct," Ramon explained. "We like to know what's going down around here. Who'd they say it was, Jas—kids?"

"Uh-huh."

"Damn howler could have its teeth in their necks, they'd blame it on kids." Ramon took an uncertain step toward Jasmine.

"You hurt yourself?" Tom noticed a flicker of concern on Jasmine's face.

"I broke my ankle, babe."

"Sure, you did. Twisted it, maybe."

"I'm hurt bad."

"Whatever." Jasmine folded her arms, turned, and, like Polar before her, disappeared through the door into the next room.

"See?" Ramon grinned at Tom. "She loves me."

He limped across the ruined kitchen and, with an exchange of nervous glances, Tom and Kate followed.

The kitchen led into a large room painted blood-red, with boarded-up windows. It was lit by a collection of mismatched lamps, lined up in a row along the opposite wall. Cigarette smoke clouded the room, and the bulbs seemed to glow fiercer through the haze, like streetlights in fog.

Six or seven people were slumped on cushions or on one of the two battered leather couches ranged in front of an enormous wide-screen TV showing highlights from a Giants game. One kid, a little smaller than Tom's kid brother, Joe, was kneeling right in front of it, close enough to count the pixels on the screen. He was shirtless, with grubby-looking bandages wrapped around his shoulder blades. Polar crept up behind the boy with his camera and snapped the back of his head.

"These are my people," Ramon told him and Kate, almost like he was challenging the two of them to disapprove.

Various grunts, calls, and gestures issued in

greeting from the slack bodies in the room as they realized Ramon was back.

But the most enthusiastic reaction came from the little figure with his nose pressed to the TV. "Ro!" he shouted, and bounded over.

"My brother, Rico," Ramon announced proudly, knocking knuckles with the kid. "Hey, could we smoke less in here?" he called to the others. "You know how it messes with Rico's asthma."

"Ain't nothing wrong with me, Ro," protested Rico fiercely.

"Sorry, man," called a big guy whose bruised face and resigned tone suggested his life was one long losing battle. "So, how'd it go?"

"Not good, Puff," Ramon told him. "They're not interested in banding up. They 'wolf now."

Puff nodded like he'd known all along and turned back to the game without another word.

Rico looked up at Kate. "The white girl's pretty," he observed.

"You think so?" Tom said, mock frowning.

"Know so." Rico grinned. His cheekbones were so high and sharp you could cut your finger on them.

"Nice TV," Tom observed.

"Cicero found it and brought it home," said Rico, pointing to a stocky, muscular kid with shades and a ponytail, spread-eagled over a large cushion.

"He found it?"

Ramon snickered. "Sure, he did. Behind an ex-rental store on 106th."

"How'd you hurt yourself, Rico?" Kate asked him, gesturing to his bandages.

Rico looked away, seeming suddenly afraid.

Ramon leaned in close to talk to Kate, as if trying to exclude Tom. "Howlers," he said. "There was some fighting when the Marqueta gang got turned. One of them nearly took off Rico's shoulder." He swore. "Kid's just ten and they done that to him. And the Marquetas are Puerto Ricans, for chrissake. We should be brothers."

Rico shrugged and drifted off back to the wide screen.

"They *bit* him?" Tom watched Rico sit back down. "Then . . . isn't he 'wolf?"

Ramon glared at him. "My brother ain't a howler. He got sick for a while, but he never turned. You should have seen the 'wolf that bit him. Went off screaming, all this froth coming out his mouth . . . It was awesome."

Rico grinned. "Guess my blood don't taste very good."

"He's a resister," Tom noted.

"You got it," Ramon said. "He's littler than you, but you ain't that strong, huh, wolf boy?"

"I didn't turn without a fight," Tom muttered. "Now, I think maybe you should tell us what's been happening around here."

"I got to take care of this ankle," Ramon said. "Come on." He hobbled into the next room. The walls there were covered with graffiti.

Tom and Kate followed him. The view brightened for Tom as Jasmine came back into sight. She was swigging from a carton of milk, leaning against a refrigerator that was so big it half obscured the doorway next to it. To keep the exit usable, the door had been taken off and a long green curtain hung there instead.

On the worktop beside the refrigerator was a battered police car radio unit, electronic entrails spilling out of its casing. A black power cord had been lashed up to its side, snaking into a socket, and the radio squawked quietly to itself like some deranged electronic parrot.

Seeing Kate, Jasmine slunk off to the opposite corner of the room, her nose wrinkling as if she'd smelled something bad. Kate pretended not to notice, but Tom saw a faint blush of color in her cheeks.

Ramon pulled off his Nikes and rested his bare foot on the table. His ankle was puffy and dark. "Get me some ice, girl, and make it better, huh?"

Jasmine snorted. "I look like your mama?" All the same, she opened the freezer door and started rummaging around inside.

He grinned at Tom and mouthed, "She loves me."

Kate shot Tom a despairing glance. "So, Ramon, you were going to tell us—"

"I told you the 'wolves were recruiting," he announced abruptly. "Takapa. His people are taking the street kids, the gangs, the homeless—all the pissed-off poor people in this city—and turning them 'wolf."

"Turning them against each other," Jasmine added, slipping a handful of ice cubes into a bowl. "Breaking old ties, old loyalties."

Kate looked at her. "And these people agree to be . . . recruited?"

"A lot of them do. Ain't no one else offering them anything." Jasmine smiled, showing the gap in her front teeth. "Guess a girl like you wouldn't know what it's like to be invisible."

"You don't know anything about me," Kate said, her green eyes flashing.

"All I got to do is look at you." Jasmine turned and disappeared through the green curtain. She came back holding a battered square can and took out some Band-Aids, cotton balls, and bandages. "What are you two even doing here, slumming with us?"

"Lay off," Ramon told her. "They're running from the howlers like we are."

"Takapa captured us both, but we got away," Tom explained. "He wants us. Bad."

Jasmine's wide brown eyes seemed just a touch wider. Tom found himself grimly satisfied at a point scored.

"What'd you do to piss off Takapa?" she demanded.

"Oh . . . stuff," Kate said levelly. "Probably safer for you if you don't know." Swiftly she changed the subject. "So these kids that Takapa's agents are approaching, they actually *want* to be 'wolf?"

Ramon shrugged. "Not like they got much choice."

"You seem to have made *your* choice," Tom said.

"There's nine of us here. Nine." Ramon was looking at Tom like he knew nothing. "We used to be a gang of almost thirty. This whole building used to be ours, not just one lousy floor."

Jasmine wrapped the ice in a cloth and passed it over to Ramon. "Some moved away when Swagger came around the first time. And some ran out on us to take up with him and the howlers."

Kate frowned. "Swagger?"

"He's running things till Takapa comes back," said Ramon, grimacing as he held the ice to his swollen ankle. "So he says."

"Swagger couldn't have cared less about us at first," Jasmine went on. "We weren't a threat. Then Ramon tried to get some of the gangs together to stand up to Swagger."

Tom nodded. "And so suddenly you *became* a threat. And I guess you can't go to the police, get their protection?"

"Nah. Just like *you* can't." Ramon looked at him pointedly. "That's why so many are getting turned now. These kids know they'll get it worse from the

27

cops than they will from the 'wolves. Running from home, running from this and from that . . . They got nowhere to go."

"And no one to turn to," Kate murmured. "So they just give up and take that bite."

Jasmine shrugged. "These people, they've felt weak all their lives. If they choose Takapa, they get strong overnight. Then they're not victims. They're the hunters."

Tom shuddered.

Kate was baffled. "What is Takapa doing?" she questioned. "Traditionally, the lupine community has always been careful about who it turns and who is chosen to continue family lines. If numbers swell too fast, the community risks drawing attention to itself. But Takapa doesn't seem to care about any of that."

"Maybe he knows he's not going to get the traditional lupines behind him," Tom suggested.

"So he's building his own power base here—however he can?" Kate nodded. "Maybe. But Jasmine, you said he was turning the 'wolves against each other?"

"That's the word out there," Jasmine replied. "I've heard that sometimes, they all get together and fight. Like in *Fight Club*—except it's a fight to the death."

Tom stared at her. "But why?"

"Hey!" shouted Rico from the next room. "The pretty white girl's on TV!"

Tom and Kate stared at each other.

"Come see, come see!" yelled Rico.

They went through the smoky fog of the TV room. Someone had flicked channels to the news. The mute symbol shone bright and blocky in the top right of the screen, obscuring Kate's picture.

Tom felt the blood drain from his head. He stumbled forward, stepping over people and pillows to get closer to the TV. Now his parents' faces were filling the screen. The camera pulled back to reveal that they were seated on a stage at what looked like a press conference.

Beside them sat Hal and Marcie Folan, Kate's parents.

He heard Kate swear. "Jesus, what is this?"

"Puff, hit the volume," Ramon snapped.

". . . Anderson, originally believed to have drowned in Seattle in mid-August in a tragic accident, and Seattle resident Kate Folan are both wanted for questioning in connection with a double homicide in New Orleans."

Two faces were flashed up, those of a broadfaced Inuit type and a shriveled old man. Tom felt his world tilt. Both men had been in the pay of Takapa. Together they'd nearly killed Tom. But then Kate's mother had arrived on the scene and killed both men so she could have Tom herself. He'd only escaped with his life thanks to Adam Blood.

But clearly Marcie was now putting her murders to further use.

The TV cameras came in for a close-up on Marcie and Hal. Flashbulbs popped and glared from the front rows of the conference.

"Whatever you've done, whatever drove you to do it," Marcie said, her voice weak with false emotion, "Tom, Kate, we ask that you give yourselves up now. . . ."

Hal nodded. The grief on his face looked real enough.

As Marcie looked into the camera, Tom felt like she was staring directly into his own eyes. "The consequences if you don't will be so much worse," she continued. Another flash went off, but Tom knew that wasn't the cause of the unmistakable spark of gold that spun through Marcie's eyes.

A different camera, placed to the side of the stage, zoomed in on Carrie Anderson, Tom's mother. He hadn't seen her for almost two months, but she seemed to have aged about ten years. She looked gray and haggard.

"Tom," she sobbed, "I don't know how we can survive this unless you come back to us soon. Please!"

Marcie moved into the shot, placing a comforting hand on Carrie's shoulder.

With a casual glance at the camera, she licked her lips.

CHAPTER THREE

The news anchorman wound things up by announcing that Kate and Tom were rumored to be in New York City.

Tom turned to Kate. "Jesus! What the hell do we do now?"

Deathly pale, Kate looked at him. Her eyes were glassy with tears. "I don't know," she replied, her voice coming out brittle and high. "I don't know *what* we do now."

"Mom and Dad thinking I was dead was bad enough, but—a murderer . . . ?" Tom paused, too choked up to continue.

Ramon looked at him hard. "Did you really waste those guys?"

"No!" Tom shouted. "They were trying to kill me! One was a 'wolf, the other was some maniac trying to cut me open—"

Kate crossed over to him and put her hands on his shoulders, trying to calm him down. "It's okay, Tom. It's okay. We have to think why she's doing this."

"She's going to kill my family," Tom whispered. He felt like he might puke. "It's a revenge thing; it must be."

Kate tried to lose the tremor in her voice. "She won't kill them. Not yet. She's using them, trying to scare you into the open." She wiped her eyes with the back of her hand. "Mom must've gotten tired of chasing us. Why waste time tracking us down when she can bring us scurrying out?"

"She wants you to go running to the cops?" Jasmine clearly didn't buy it. "Why? How would she get you then?"

"The cops don't just *know* about the 'wolves," Kate told her sharply. "Some of them *are* 'wolves. The lupine community can only survive if blind eyes are turned in some pretty high places—so a whole lot of 'wolves make it their duty to climb to the top of the career ladder of all the useful professions. Police, politics, medicine . . ."

Jasmine nodded slowly. "So if you give yourselves up to the cops, what happens?"

"We'll meet with some kind of accident," Tom said. "Or maybe we'll 'escape' and never be found again. Get my drift?"

"Well, whatever," said Ramon. "You two are trouble. And we got enough crap going down here without you two bringing your own."

Kate glared at him. "This is the thanks we get for saving your life?"

"It's okay, Kate," Tom said quietly. "They're just scared. We can't blame them for that."

"Yo, Ramon," drawled Cicero, from where he lay stretched out on the floor. "Maybe we should let Takapa have 'em if the howlers want 'em so bad."

There was a heavy pause. Tom glanced around the room, steeling himself for fight or flight. All eyes were on him and Kate.

But Ramon shook his head. "Takapa don't do deals. Even if he did, we don't trade with howlers." He turned to Jasmine. "Here's the deal. Rico needs his bandages changed; it's time he got to Woollard's place. Jasmine, you'll take him in the morning, huh?"

Jasmine nodded. "Sure."

Ramon turned back to Tom and Kate. "This dude Woollard used to be a doctor," he explained. "He helps us out. We help *him* out. He knows about the 'wolves, even treats some of their victims. Maybe he knows the dude you came here to find. Jasmine, babe, take them with you, okay?"

Jasmine was about to open her mouth as if to argue when several loud thumps at the door rumbled through the room. Jasmine took a couple of nimble steps back in alarm. Rico hit the mute on the TV, then jumped for cover behind one of the couches. The others held themselves still as statues except for Polar, who rose automatically—ready to take a snap of their mystery visitors.

Ramon blocked his way. "Sit down. You think that's the mailman out there or something? It's almost four a.m."

Kate edged closer to Tom. He felt her icy fingers coil into his own and squeezed her hand tightly.

There were two more loud knocks, then nothing. The silence continued for what must have been a full minute. People began to breathe again.

Then, with a hideous splintering noise, the front door was smashed in.

The room erupted into movement as people scrambled up from the floor or their couches, swearing and yelling. Tom and Kate backed away involuntarily, knocking against one of the lamps.

Ramon turned to Jasmine. "Get the gun," he told her, but she was already running for the other room. He pulled a switchblade from his jacket pocket just as a giant in biker's leather burst into their hideout, wielding a sledgehammer. He had a pale, dangerous-looking face. His hair was a greasy crown of thick blond spikes. His heavy-lidded gray eyes sparked with reckless aggression, and his teeth were bared in a wild grin. Scores of tiny boils festered in the chapped, red skin around his mouth.

"Hey, kids!" The man laughed. "Ain'tcha got milk and cookies for Swagger?"

Before anyone could react, Swagger brought the hammer's heavy wooden handle up under Ramon's chin. There was a loud crack and the boy reeled backward. Puff lumbered toward their uninvited guest, fists raised, but Swagger shoved him aside, sending him sprawling over the couch to land heavily in front of the TV.

Tom tried to help Ramon get up, but the big man turned, grabbed a fistful of Tom's dark hair, and threw him aside. Tom landed in a heap at Kate's feet, gasping as he banged his head on a sharp corner.

Swagger took two long steps into the room. Two big guys—one black, one white, both dressed in ragged denim over black leather, biker style—followed him inside, armed with baseball bats.

"Anyone else want to play?" Swagger inquired.

Jasmine burst out from the other room. Both her hands were clamped hard around a gun. "Don't make me use this," she said carefully.

A slow grin spread over Swagger's face. "Aw, is the little girl gonna pop us?"

Ramon reached up from where he lay and wrangled the gun from Jasmine's stiff grip.

Swagger took a step forward, but Ramon quickly fired over his head. The noise was deafening, and plaster rained down like confetti over Swagger and his sidekicks. His smug expression turned sour.

Struggling to his feet, Ramon held his gun arm rigid and pointed at Swagger's head. "Take off."

Swagger remained still but gestured with his eyes first at Tom, then at Kate, who shifted uncomfortably under his stare. "So who's this? Reinforcements?"

"They're nobody," said Ramon.

"Figures, if they hang with you."

Ramon jerked the gun. "What did you come here for, Swagger?"

Swagger let his gaze linger on Kate a moment longer. Then he looked at Ramon. "I'm giving you one last chance. Takapa wants you all at the arena, midnight Friday."

"Why?"

"To show your allegiance."

"We got no allegiance to him," said Ramon. "Just to each other."

"You think we're stupid?" added Jasmine. "We go down there, we're dead."

"You got Papa Takapa all wrong," Swagger said. "He wants you to come and *party* on Friday. And he's offering 'wolf *protection*. He wants to look out for you."

Ramon scowled. "We got all we need right here."

"Yeah?" Swagger smiled nastily. "Not for long."

As if he'd been signaled, the big black guy hurled his baseball bat at Jasmine, who yelped and fell back. Ramon turned instinctively toward her, and Swagger kicked the gun from his hand. The other intruder brought his own bat down on Ramon's head.

"No!" screamed Rico.

Then everything seemed to happen at once. The guy who'd brought down Ramon swung his bat into the TV. Rico yelled as the glass shattered and white sparks spewed out.

Kate crouched down to help Tom up. "Come on, there must be a back way out of here," she hissed.

Tom was still dazed. He saw Cicero try to tackle the man with the bat, leaping on his back. But Swagger grabbed Cicero by the neck and threw him against the wall.

Two of Ramon's friends had clearly decided not to stick around. They jumped over Cicero's body and fled the same way Swagger had come in.

"Fleet, China, get back here!" yelled Jasmine. She had picked up the bat that had been thrown at her and was wielding it like she meant business. But the black guy had grabbed Ramon's gun. He brought it up ready to fire at her.

Kate cursed, leaned past Tom, and yanked the lamp plug out of the wall.

The place was plunged into blackness.

All movement stopped. The only sound was a low, male voice, Cicero maybe: *Por favor, no me muerda.* Don't bite me," again and again.

Before Tom's eyes could even begin to adjust, Kate was dragging him up to his feet. "Move," she said fiercely. "Refrigerator room. Maybe there's an exit behind that green curtain."

Tom charged into the room with the refrigerator but collided with the table. The sound of bottles and glasses toppling filled the air.

"Stop them!" Swagger ordered.

A shot was fired. Tom heard Kate cry out—in alarm, he hoped, not pain.

Footsteps were coming toward him. Tom was on all fours, disoriented now, groping for the green curtain. His mind was clouding; he could feel the 'wolf bucking inside his body. He struggled to hold on. If he lost control now, lashed out in the dark, how could he hope to tell friend from foe?

Someone knocked into him in passing. "Kate?" The curtain billowed out into his face as someone swept it aside. Tom grabbed a fistful of the fabric, got up, and felt his way through into the space beyond.

He found himself in a filthy room lit by the sputtering flames of three stubby candles. Tom stared around, trying to get his bearings. A pair of moldy mattresses had been slung on the floor, bunched-up sleeping bags beside them. A closet door hung open on a single hinge. Perhaps he could hide there until—

Too late. One of Swagger's heavies came charging inside, the black one with the gun. Tom tripped him and the guy went crashing to the ground, snuffing out two of the candles as he fell.

Another shape stole into the room. Tom could just about make out that it was female. "Kate?" he hissed, his heart thumping wildly. "That you?"

"Shut your stupid mouth and follow me," Jasmine hissed back, crossing to the closet.

Now Tom could see that the wall at the back of it had been knocked through.

"Emergency exit, huh?"

"Got to be prepared. Cops, 'wolves . . . everyone wants a piece of us."

"Where does it lead?"

"Next door," muttered Jasmine. "Rico came this way. He's sick with his asthma. We gotta get after him."

"You go," Tom told her. "I'm going back to find Kate."

Jasmine was squeezing her body through the hole in the wall. "She already got chased out the front way with Ramon, I think."

The fallen thug was rising, a low growl building in his throat. A sudden feral stench filled the room, along with the sound of heavy stitching ripping apart. He was turning 'wolf, Tom realized. A shot of excitement tore through him. He shook his head. He *had* to hold on. . . . He could control it—he was a wereling, wasn't he?

"Get in here!" Jasmine hissed at him.

The thug was no longer human. He was a dark, crouched, misshapen figure, panting and snapping his heavy jaws.

Tom darted for the closet door while the creature was still disoriented. He gasped as he landed heavily on the damp debris that littered the floor.

Jasmine helped him up.

"Jas, is that you?" Rico sounded lost and small

39

somewhere in the darkness ahead. His hoarse breath had an unsettling rasp to it.

"Stay still, Rico. We're coming."

"Where's Ramon?" He broke into a coughing fit.

Jasmine shushed him desperately. "What happened to your inhaler?" she demanded.

"Didn't work," Rico gasped between awful, whooping coughs. "Threw it away."

"Jesus, Rico," Jasmine began—then an exultant roar sounded behind them.

Tom spun around to find that the werewolf had pushed its great, bestial head through the hole in the wall. He saw the sick yellow gleam of its eyes, turning this way and that around the ruined room.

"Out of here!" shouted Jasmine, scooping up Rico in her arms and running toward the only chinks of light in the darkness. "This way!"

But the doorway was boarded up. Behind it Tom heard masonry crumble under the the 'wolf's massive paws.

Tom gestured at the planks. "*This* is prepared?"

Jasmine turned and dumped Rico onto him. The kid locked his arms around Tom's neck, shaking and wheezing, and the two of them watched as Jasmine knocked two of the planks out with a few savage kicks.

"They're only tacked over the window," she muttered. "What, you want *anyone* getting in?"

"It's us getting *out* I'm worried about," Tom replied, kicking the last two planks away himself.

A split second later Jasmine was leading the way out into the cold, dark street. Tom followed close behind, panting with the exertion of carrying Rico.

"We've got to find Kate," he hissed at her. "Is there a place you meet up again after a bust or—"

"Rico's really sick," Jasmine snapped, crossing over to a beat-up old Cadillac across the street. "We need transport."

The kid was squirming and coughing in Tom's arms, struggling for breath. "He's having an asthma attack?"

"It happened before. He nearly died. Little idiot won't use his inhaler." Somehow she'd forced open the driver's door of the Cadillac and now she was busy working at the wiring inside.

Tom watched her. "Wait a second—you're stealing that car?"

"Guess I am," she said dryly. "Hey, do you think Jesus will still want me for a sunbeam?"

The hunting roar of the 'wolf floated eerily down the dark street, and Tom cast an anxious glance back over his shoulder. "We might find out sooner than you think."

The Cadillac suddenly growled into life. "Get over here," Jasmine insisted. "We gotta get to Doc Woollard's, fast."

Tom opened the rear door and placed Rico inside. "I can't come with you," he said. "I have to find Kate."

Jasmine stared hard at him. "Get your sorry ass in this car *now*. Look at that kid! He could stop breathing. You want me to give him CPR while I'm driving?"

Tom heard the sound of heavy lupine footfalls tearing down the asphalt, saw a dark, massive blur moving up behind him.

"In!" Jasmine shouted.

Tom ducked inside and Jasmine was speeding away before he'd even shut the door. Rico was struggling for breath, his eyes bulging as the coughs kept coming. Through the rear windshield Tom watched grimly as the hideous creature pelted after them, huge head low to the road like it was scenting the exhaust.

Up ahead was a red light, and a big truck blocked their way. Jasmine cursed as she hit the brakes.

Tom was thrown forward. Rico gripped tightly onto his hand, wheezing and choking. Tom turned and checked on the lupine. It was almost on top of them.

"It's still coming!" he yelled.

As it readied itself to pounce, the creature opened its great jaws in triumph.

CHAPTER FOUR

Kate practically shoved Ramon along ahead of her. "You've got to keep going," she urged him, but she knew he couldn't last much longer. His ankle was bad and his head was worse. He had a sticky gash on the back of his skull from the blow with the bat. Blood had run down and soaked through the collar of his thin cotton shirt.

When he stumbled and nearly fell for about the fourteenth time, she steered him over to rest against the nearest doorway.

While Ramon caught his breath, Kate looked around for any sign of Swagger or his thugs. But the street was silent and empty.

Where was Tom? Kate could have punched the wall with frustration. She'd have been with him now if that hand hadn't curled around her ankle back in the darkened room before she could take off after him. It had been Cicero, or Puff, or one of them, sprawled and hurting on the floor—reaching out, confused, scared in the darkness.

She'd managed to pull away, but then someone small—Rico?—had pushed past her and she'd stumbled and lost her balance.

A flame had sprung from Swagger's lighter, inches from her face. Kate flinched from the heat; the big man had grabbed for her, but Ramon had recovered enough to sucker punch him. As Swagger fell backward, Ramon had grabbed hold of her and together they'd bundled out of the room through the wreck of the kitchen and the shattered front door and out into the cold, damp October night.

They'd barely gotten a block away and they'd already reached a standstill.

Ramon's dark eyes were scrunched up in pain and frustration. The scar on his cheek was ugly white against his sweaty olive complexion. "Why don't you leave me?" he muttered.

"What, and shatter your faith in human kindness?" Kate shook her head. "No, we'll just rest here for a few seconds and—"

"Don't matter, anyhow," he interrupted. "Swagger's won. My people all split, my home is smashed up. It's over."

"Your brother's out there with Jasmine and Tom," Kate told him. "They got away, I'm sure of it. They'll be back."

"Well, well," a low, unpleasant voice called out. "Didn't get very far, did you?"

"Looks like someone else is back first," muttered Ramon.

Kate felt her stomach sinking into her shoes. She turned to find Swagger standing at the end of the street with one of his "little helpers." The streetlight overhead cast a sick sodium glare over his zombie complexion, making him look even nastier than before.

"I ain't going down like this," hissed Ramon, bunching his fists.

"Very macho," Kate breathed.

"Come on, little girl," Swagger called. "We ain't finished talking to you yet."

Kate realized that Ramon, sunk back in the doorway, must be hidden from Swagger's view. "Stay here, rest, get back to your hideout," she whispered. "I'll lead them away."

She turned and attempted to saunter down the empty street toward Swagger. "The reason I didn't go very far," she announced, "was so that you wouldn't take so long to catch up with me."

Swagger looked at her, hooded gray eyes beady with suspicion. "Is that a fact?"

"Yep," Kate said, forcing herself to look up at him and smile. "Those losers tried to make me go with them. But I prefer to be on the winners' side."

Swagger smiled. "Winners' side is the howlers' side. You like 'wolves?"

"Uh . . . sure." She nodded.

45

A different gleam came into Swagger's eyes. "Just who are you, sweetheart? You don't look Ramon's type."

Kate shrugged. "Don't know him. Me and my friend were just hanging."

A grin spread over Swagger's face. "I got a better idea. Why don't you come back with me tonight?"

Kate willed her smile not to shrivel and die. "But it's almost morning."

Swagger nodded excitedly. "And the action kicks off at dawn. My soldiers have been getting psyched all night. Soon they get to play." He took her by the wrist and led her away.

"Where are we going?" she asked, trying to sound casual.

"Oh, baby," said Swagger. "You'll find out soon enough."

"Here it comes!" Tom shouted to Jasmine. The drooling 'wolf leapt through the air, claws outstretched, ready to smash its way through the rear windshield to get them.

With a wordless grunt Jasmine revved the engine and the car shot forward, Jasmine yanking hard on the wheel to avoid the truck in front.

The 'wolf fell short of them, skidding to a halt, its claws raking up the asphalt. It howled in anger as its prey moved out of reach.

Tom winced as they almost hit a car coming the

other way. It swerved and crashed into a row of trash cans.

Jasmine ran the red light, then swerved hard to the left to avoid a delivery van taking the corner. It blared its horn. But the 'wolf was back up and running for them.

Tom could feel his own change starting to rise up inside him, more insistent than ever. The fear, the panic, the craving for release seemed to have been pumping and pounding through his veins for hours, wearing away his human self. He could taste the sharp tang of blood at the back of his throat and his mouth was flooding with saliva.

"That thing's not giving up!" he shouted.

"Me neither," Jasmine replied calmly. Wheels screeched and rubber burned as she steered the car around in a tight arc.

Tom saw the delivery truck screech to a halt as the dark shape of the 'wolf bolted out in front of it and caught a glancing blow. At the next block Jasmine took a left and floored it, and the carnage was hidden from view.

Tom felt the tension that racked his body lose a little of its grip. He realized he'd been holding his breath. He unclenched his fists and saw that his palms were scored with nail marks. The taste of blood at the back of his throat soured, turning his stomach. The danger of the change taking hold was fading. For now.

"I think we lost the 'wolf," he said shakily.

Jasmine nodded, apparently satisfied.

Rico had stopped coughing and was breathing a little easier now, in shallow wheezes. Tom squeezed his hand. "It's okay," he told the kid. "Everything will be fine soon." For a second he could almost make believe he was talking to Joe, riding through the night to Seattle in the back of Dad's old Chrysler before this whole nightmare started.

He thought back to the press conference on TV. Now his whole family was snared in Marcie Folan's twisted plans . . . and where the hell was Kate? He shut his eyes, wished he could think of some clean way through all this.

"You falling asleep back there?" Jasmine inquired.

He sighed. "I can't imagine ever sleeping again."

"Good. 'Cause now we gotta go wake up Doc Woollard and get Rico fixed up. Then we can check back with the crew and your girlfriend. Okay?"

Tom just nodded, feeling a strange unease that went beyond the horror they'd just experienced. Jasmine had just seen her home wrecked and her friends beaten up, been shot at and then chased by a hungry 'wolf. Yet here she was, driving along in her stolen car, so calm and so in control. Taking it all in stride. He couldn't help but shudder. Just what did you have to live through to get that way?

•   •   •

"This is our rink," said Swagger proudly, leading the way down the central aisle through the tiers of seating. "Shaun, stay on security."

"Check." Shaun the bodyguard stayed by the exit doors but gestured that Kate should follow Swagger down into the auditorium.

Kate did her best to look impressed as she stared around the ruined expanse, hidden away beneath a derelict warehouse building on East 91st Street. It was hard to believe this dilapidated, echoing arena had ever been an actual ice rink, a place of brightness and music and fun. Now its surface was damp, grimy concrete, spattered and stained with stubborn pools of dried blood. Dim lights burned high above the endless, empty seating, casting distorted shadows over the arena. If there was any ice left in the place, it must have been in the air; each breath Kate took chilled her insides, then ghosted out of her mouth in a fine cloud of freezing mist.

Swagger eased himself onto the front row of rotting wooden benches and looked at her expectantly.

"So," she managed at last, "this is all yours, huh?"

"It's Takapa's." Swagger's chest puffed up with pride. "But I run the events here."

"Just who is this Takapa?" she asked. She couldn't let Swagger think she knew anything.

"Maybe I'll introduce you. I think he'd like you."

Kate tried to keep the alarm from her voice. "He's coming here?"

Swagger nodded. "Tonight."

"Tonight . . . Well. Cool."

Swagger looked at her strangely. "You all right, honey?"

Sure, she thought. *I can't wait to say hi again to the murdering freak I screwed over. The murdering freak who wants to get with me.* The temperature suddenly seemed a couple of degrees colder, and she knew she had to change the subject. "You seem to know Ramon's people. Were you part of their gang?"

"Had a girl once who was," said Swagger. "I used to hang with them sometimes."

"When you were just human?" she asked lightly.

He spat on the floor. "When I was nothing."

Suddenly the door above them was flung open with a crash. A half-dressed black man greeted Shaun and then came down the steps. As he approached, Kate recognized him as Swagger's other sidekick from Ramon's place.

Swagger didn't seem impressed to see him wearing only a pair of ill-fitting trousers. "You went 'wolf on them?" he said quietly. "You lost control?"

The man looked furious but said nothing.

"Takapa said not to kill them," Swagger went on. "You kill them, Eric?"

The big man shook his head. "Lost them. The little kid, the white boy, and that bitch Jasmine."

Swagger looked at Kate sharply. "Seems your boyfriend's got some new buddies."

It was all Kate could do not to collapse with relief. Instead she just shrugged, kept her face neutral. "That's cool. So do I."

He nodded at her, then turned a more critical look on the black guy. "You lost control, Eric. I don't know if I can trust you on my personal staff no more."

Eric held himself stiffly. "Sorry."

Swagger fixed him with a cold stare. "Tell you what. Why don't you go get our gladiators down here?"

Eric turned to obey, but as he walked down onto the floor of the rink, Swagger called to him again. "Oh, and Eric? I want you to fight down there. For me, huh?"

Eric froze for a moment. Then he walked on without turning around. The heavy slaps of his bare feet on the concrete sounded around the arena, lingering long after he'd been swallowed up by the shadows.

Swagger patted the bench beside him.

Kate forced herself to sit beside him. "What did you mean, gladiators?" she asked casually.

"I'm an emperor here," Swagger said. "We bring people here to fight. Fight for their lives."

Kate knew he was watching her, but she couldn't meet his stare. "For your entertainment?"

"You don't think that's a good enough reason?" Swagger slipped an arm around her shoulders. It was all Kate could do not to cringe. "Nah. This ain't about bloodlust. Not just bloodlust, anyway. We got big plans." He grinned nastily. "Let me tell you, babe, there's going to be some changes coming to this city. Everything's going to be up for grabs, and me and my boys are getting a *big* share." Then he looked at her meaningfully and added in a softer voice, "Everything we want is going to be ours to take."

Kate forced a weak smile, but her mind was a whirl. Just what was it that Takapa was planning? Since her mother was here in New York too, chances were she was involved in it somehow. Marcie had been impressed with Takapa when they'd met in New Orleans. Whatever. If Swagger wasn't just shooting his mouth off and Takapa really *was* coming here sometime soon—with or without her mom in tow—Kate knew she was in mortal danger.

Like that's anything new, she thought bitterly.

Swagger's sweaty fingers caressed the side of her neck. She wanted to gag and thanked God when a sudden clatter echoed out across the arena and he pulled away.

Swagger's attention switched to the old rink. He rubbed his hands together with childish glee. "Here they come."

Just as Kate had been feeling that no further tension could be wrung from her body, the sight she saw made every muscle tense up, every nerve jangle. Eric was leading ten people, none of them older than thirty, into the middle of the arena. Their footfalls built from a murmur to a rumble. Some were clutching themselves, either against the cold or with fear. Others marched along almost jauntily.

There were all kinds of people there. Junkie types, pencil thin with gaunt faces. Average Joes in jeans and sweaters, staring around glumly in resigned expectation. A couple of muscle-bound types in plaid shirts. And there were two women in the little crowd, looking about edgily: one short haired and stocky, in denim, the other a hard-faced blonde with ratted hair, her neck spiderwebbed with tattoos.

There was something about the way they moved that was slightly unfocused, jumpy—like they were coming down from taking something.

Eric sorted them roughly into two sides, picking out people and propelling them across the concrete floor to stand together, each group facing the other. The echoes faded as they all stood still as statues, like they were trying to stare each other down in the murky light.

"You expect them to start fighting?" Kate whispered. "Just like that?"

"They got no choice." Swagger chuckled. "Let the combat begin, y'all!" he yelled.

With the words still ringing around the auditorium, Eric lurched into action. First he pushed one of the average Joes in the first group down, then he took a swing at the stocky woman on the opposing side. She cried out and went down. Some of the others eyed each other nervously. One of the junkie types just stared down at his feet, clutching his head like this nightmare would all go away if he only wished hard enough.

No chance. Eric whacked him in the stomach, doubling him over.

Kate looked away, her stomach twisting, but every new shout and cry tugged her reluctant gaze back. The violence unfolded in a series of sickening snapshots. The junkie collapsing to the concrete, clutching his head . . . the average Joe running to kick him while he was down . . . the blond girl raking her nails down a muscleman's face . . . the stocky woman grabbing her by the throat.

"Come on!" yelled Swagger. "You're not even trying! I know what you need, people. Whoever brings Eric down gets double!"

"*What* do they need?" Kate asked him.

Swagger wasn't listening. He breathed in deep. "Work together now! Good job!" He clapped his big hand down hard on Kate's shoulder. "Don't it make you feel good?"

You're mad, thought Kate. *You're truly insane.* But she could only sit there helplessly as the fighting grew wilder and bloodier.

CHAPTER FIVE

Jasmine banged on Dr. Woollard's door so hard that Tom thought she might put her fist right through it. He checked his watch: almost 6 a.m. Rico was leaning on him drowsily. In the car the kid had kept falling into a fitful sleep, only to wake himself again by coughing.

They had ditched the stolen car a couple of blocks away, and Jasmine had led the way to a shabby-looking brownstone on the fringes of Harlem, overlooking a vacant lot.

"Do you often come calling so early?" Tom asked as Jasmine knocked even harder.

"He don't exactly keep office hours," she said. "And he ain't always strictly sober. But he's plenty smart. Supposed to be a genius." She frowned. "Least, he was once."

Tom heard a grumbling voice coming toward the door.

"All right, all right. I'm coming. . . ." A bolt was thrown, then another, then a third. Finally the door opened to reveal a singularly unimpressive little man, half dressed in a lumpy brown cardigan with nothing beneath it and a pair of striped pajama bottoms.

He stared out at them blearily. His gray hair was mussed up in a dozen different directions, a wild frame for his lined and haggard face. There was a droopy look about him, as if his face and body were giving up to gravity even as you watched. But his eyes were an arresting amber color. They transfixed you, even clouded by sleep and drink and God knew what else.

"Hey, Doc," said Jasmine. "We need you to take a look at Rico."

Woollard glanced down at the boy, then back to Jasmine. "Okay, I've seen him. Now would you mind leaving me in peace?" His voice was gravelly, but he had a refined accent, British, maybe.

Jasmine seemed unfazed. "He's got a howler bite, Doc, remember?"

Woollard knitted his brows together as if trying to recall. "Rico . . . bite . . ." He snapped his fingers and swayed drunkenly in the doorway. "Yes, of course. Rico, our little resister. Very interesting . . ."

"He just had a real bad asthma attack, too, choking, no breath," Jasmine persisted.

Woollard seemed to lose interest and began mumbling to himself. "I'm going back to bed," he announced grumpily.

"Please?" Jasmine opened her beautiful eyes as wide as they'd go. "I did bring you a real big bottle of JD last time." She smiled craftily. "And I might again."

Woollard's eyes lit up. "Perhaps I *am* being a little ungracious," he said. "Come inside." With that he turned and shambled from view.

Jasmine ushered Rico inside, then turned to Tom. "As doctors go, he's cheap."

Tom frowned. "He looks like he could use a little medical attention himself. You're really going to let him examine Rico while he's in that state?"

"Listen, the sooner we get Rico checked out, the sooner we get you back to your girlfriend, okay?"

Tom couldn't fault that logic and followed her into the squalid little apartment. It reeked of whiskey and garlic, and there must have been a dozen crucifixes arranged on the walls of the entrance hall. "He's expecting vampires?" Tom asked quietly.

Jasmine pulled out a cell phone. "When you've drunk as much as he has, guess you don't know *what* you're gonna see next."

Tom nodded to the phone. "Are you calling Ramon?"

Jasmine shook her head. "He lost his cell phone in the park, remember? Anyhow, I got no credit left. Incoming calls only." She hit some keys and waited. Then she sighed. "No messages."

Woollard was rooting around in a ramshackle

room that was part office, part living room. A bare lightbulb dangled down from the ceiling, so low that Tom nearly banged his head on it. He stepped carefully; the floor was barely visible under piles of clutter and scattered papers. The walls were covered in arcane astrological charts, wax-sealed scrolls, and ancient-looking pieces of parchment packed with strange scrawls in stranger languages. Incongruous amid all this mystical bric-a-brac was a dog-eared certificate in a dirty frame: Woollard's doctorate in science from Yale University. The document had been signed almost thirty years ago and looked as battered and faded now as the man himself.

Tom wondered what had happened to the scholar to bring him as low as this dank, stinking apartment. Suddenly he felt lonely. It was still dark through the open blinds, and he wondered where Kate was right now. Weird. He used to think first of his family when he felt low. Now it was Kate's face that swam into his mind: that look on her face, soft and serious at the same time. . . .

With a grunt of satisfaction Woollard finally found what he was looking for: a dirty glass. He poured himself a generous measure of Jack Daniels, then drained the glass in one gulp. "I'm sorry that I can't offer you any," he said, looking at Jasmine and Rico in turn, "but you're not twenty-one." Then he squinted at Tom, as if noticing him for the first time. "Who is this?" he asked Jasmine.

"A friend," she answered.

Tom felt vaguely flattered. "My name's Tom," he added.

Woollard poured himself another drink. "You've noticed my unusual interior decorations?"

"They're, uh, a little hard to miss," Tom confirmed.

"And now you think I'm just a pathetic old lush who hangs garlic around his windows and uses black magic to shore up his ruins, hmm?"

"No, sir," Tom said uneasily.

Woollard fixed him with those burning eyes. It was like they alone held his vitality and the rest of his body had quietly withered away around them. "There are many dark things in this city," he said. "Phantoms and fiends and creatures of the night. I've heard them, seen them. I've seen such things. . . ." He glared suddenly at Jasmine. "Sleep does not come easy to me. These charms and doctrines, fragile though they might seem, lend me a little security."

This time he sipped from his glass and nodded appreciatively, like he'd suddenly noticed the taste. "Right, let's get down to business." He sighed and looked at Rico. "I suppose I should examine you properly, check what's what. See how that bite's healing, too . . ." he said without much enthusiasm. "You know where the examination room is."

Rico hopped off the chair and tottered back out into the hallway. Woollard followed him. "Excuse me," he said.

"And clearly you do," Tom said to Jasmine once Woollard had left the room. "Excuse him, I mean. For a lot."

She shrugged and coiled her lithe body into Woollard's old office chair. "He knows about the 'wolves. He doesn't ask questions. And he helps us all he can."

"Because you bribe him with booze."

"Stolen whiskey's cheaper than medical insurance," she said, yawning.

Tom shook his head. "I can't believe you leave Rico alone with him."

"Rico likes him. Woollard ain't no freak," said Jasmine, her dark eyes flashing. "He's just in bad times. We don't all get lucky in life, Tom."

That's for sure, thought Tom. Then he heard a voice, low and furtive sounding: Woollard. He strained to hear; he'd learned that if he focused hard enough, he was able to summon his more sensitive lupine hearing to his human form.

"I see . . ." Woollard was saying quietly. "What are your instructions?" A tinny, scratchy voice answered from the other end of a phone line, but Tom couldn't quite make out the words. "Yes, that makes sense. Can you get your hands on some?"

"Jasmine," Tom hissed. "Woollard's making a call in there. Come on, let's listen."

Though puzzled, she moved quietly as a cat, creeping out after him into the hall.

"Yes, I've got what you've been waiting for." Woollard's voice was clear enough through the door for Jasmine to hear every word. "Ready for delivery. Will you pick them up or shall I arrange for them to be delivered?"

Tom gripped Jasmine tightly by the arm. "This is a trap," he whispered. "Woollard's selling us out!"

Her face darkened. "Who to?"

"I don't know, but he's got Rico in there!" Tom pressed his ear to the examination room door but still couldn't decipher the voice on the phone. "There's only one way to find out." He gripped the handle, ready to throw open the door.

Kate felt colder than she'd ever felt in her life. A big knot had formed in her throat as she watched Eric grapple with a succession of screaming opponents. She turned to Swagger in shocked disbelief. "Isn't he supposed to be your friend?"

"Sure. But he's got a lesson to learn." He scratched the pustules around his mouth with dirty fingers. "It's okay. Eric can look after himself."

"When it's ten against one?" Kate muttered.

But Swagger seemed to be right. Eric was kicking and punching and knocking heads together like a cut-rate Jackie Chan, smashing his way through his opponents, sending them reeling.

Swagger turned to Kate. "Think we should let Eric off the hook now, baby?"

Kate stared at him helplessly. She wanted no part in this, no responsibility for what happened to any of these wretched people.

But Swagger took her silence for tacit approval. "Okay, warm-up's over. Forget Eric," Swagger commanded, "and forget any bonus. Stick with your team now. Bring down your opponents—if you want what's waiting. . . ."

What the hell *was* waiting for these people? Kate wondered. What could be worth all this?

Eric stood back, folded his burly arms, and watched as the teams regrouped, panting, clutching at wounds, wiping blood and sweat from their faces. Then they were bawling and yelling as they bundled together to fight, eyes wild and limbs flailing.

Make it stop! Kate wanted to scream at Swagger. *Stop this senseless stupidity now!* She buried her face in her hands as the fighting between the two teams grew even more savage, as the screams got louder and crimson stains bloomed on the cracked concrete floor.

Swagger started to whoop and catcall. Against her better judgment Kate found herself morbidly drawn to see why. Someone was trying to limp away from the struggle, one of the muscle-bound types—he looked like a modern-day gladiator but clearly had no stomach to play any longer. The tattooed blonde was sprawled on the ground, roaring at him to come back and fight. Her body was shaking, twitching. With horrified fascination Kate saw that a thick, pale pelt was bristling out from her darkening skin.

"It's 'wolf time," cackled Swagger.

Maybe it was the anger, the fear, the desperation that was palpable in the arena—but the woman wasn't the only one turning 'wolf. Like a yawn being passed on to someone watching, the other fighters began to change too, shucking off their humanity with their bloodied clothes, crouching and yowling. Flesh furred over. Bones and ligaments crunched and snapped as they formed anew. Lupine eyes shone the same glassy gold as the lights that burned up above.

The blond woman's lupine form was ragged, scrawny looking. Kate could see welts in the beast's back from the fighting, and one of her legs was damaged, but she could still run at a frightening speed. The muscleman didn't stand a chance. He let out a scream, then went down, his body hidden from view by the 'wolf's bulk. The grunts as she fed on her prey were amplified by the distorting acoustics in the arena.

Kate couldn't keep silent any longer. "This isn't a contest," she stormed, "it's a slaughter. *Murder!*"

"It's survival of the fittest," said Swagger. "These punks soon learn: they're stronger if they fight as a team. That's what all this is about. That's what we got to make them see."

With a chill Kate saw he was right. The human

skirmishes had been scrappy, frantic affairs, but the pack instinct was more dominant in the lupine state. The 'wolves were working together in their factions. Two of the beasts had brought down a third, their great paws pressing down on the creature's neck. Another was methodically herding its wounded opponent toward the slavering jaws of its waiting ally, blocking any attempt to pass, forcing it back.

The fight was clearly coming to an end. Two men and the stocky woman lay twisted and still in their own congealing blood. A 'wolf lay twitching on its side, barely breathing; long gashes scored the length of its body. Three victorious lupines sat hunched over their vanquished opponents, as if waiting for something.

Kate realized they were looking to Swagger.

"The choice is mine," he whispered, rapt as he drank in the carnage before him. "All I have to do is reach out my hand. . . ." He did so, extending his thumb. "I'm the judge, see? If I raise my thumb, the losers live to fight again. If I lower it—they die." He looked at Kate. "See that? Got more power in my thumb than most people get in a lifetime."

Kate saw his shadow on the stand before them. In silhouette the spikes of his hair could have been a crown of laurel leaves, just like those worn by the emperors of Rome.

"Let them live," she pleaded.

"Why should I?"

"They're your own kind. Lupines. Bound by the ties of the 'wolf brotherhood.'"

Swagger looked at Kate oddly. "You know about that old-days stuff?"

"Enough to know that 'wolves don't kill 'wolves. It's senseless; there aren't enough—"

"Not enough howlers?" Swagger shook his head. "You're wrong. Soon they'll be a dime a dozen."

"What do you mean?" Kate demanded.

Swagger's smile slipped a little, like he was aware he'd maybe said too much.

Kate swallowed hard, placed her hand on his face, and softly caressed his cheek in a desperate effort to distract him. He turned to her, confused for a moment—then smiled. A smug *I-knew-you-wanted-me* smile.

"Please," she said softly. "Whatever you're doing this for, let the losers live. Haven't enough people died?"

Swagger looked at her, shook his head a fraction. "Ain't never enough."

His thumb came down.

Kate closed her eyes and clasped her hands over her ears. But she couldn't hope to shut out the cacophony of baying and howling that filled the auditorium and echoed through the freezing air as the victors began to feed on their fallen prey.

65

CHAPTER SIX

Tom kicked open the door to Dr. Woollard's examination room. "What's going on, Doc?" he demanded. "Why the private call?"

Woollard looked at him in surprise. He held a stethoscope in one hand and an ancient cell phone the size of a brick in the other. It seemed he'd just killed the call. Rico was lying placidly on a couch, his filthy old dressings replaced with fresh bandages. He was drumming his fingers on the cracked black leather, staring at a handwritten optician's eye chart and looking bored.

"Who were you talking to?" Jasmine asked uncertainly.

"Stacy Stein at the medical center," Woollard told her, seemingly bewildered by their behavior. "I wanted her opinion on prescribing theophylline for Rico's asthma."

Tom wasn't convinced. "Aren't *you* supposed to be a doctor?"

"I'm not a general practitioner," Woollard replied

crossly, resting the phone on a cluttered workbench. "I specialize in genetics and hematology."

Jasmine screwed up her nose. "Say what?"

"Study of the blood," Woollard explained. "I led the field at Yale. But that was a long time ago," he added with a sigh. "The medicine I had in mind for Rico lists heart murmurs as a possible side effect, and since Dr. Stein is more intimately acquainted with his medical history than I, I simply sought her advice."

"Who is Stacy Stein?" Tom asked suspiciously.

"She sticks needles in you," chirped Rico, but speaking made him cough again.

"Runs programs, tests, medical trials, things like that," Jasmine added with a grimace. "She works with a whole lot of kids on the streets. Always on your case, always judging you. 'You using? You drinking?' She don't quit trying to get you straight. It's like going to see your mom or something."

"So you come to Woollard for treatment instead. I guess he's not about to give anyone a hard time about that," Tom observed. Though he couldn't agree with her preference, at least it made a bit more sense to him now. "But how come she knows Rico's medical history? She doesn't know about the 'wolves, right?"

Jasmine laughed in his face. "She knows, all right. And she knows Rico's a resister—that's why she's so hot on him."

Tom nodded thoughtfully. Before this nightmare had begun, he'd have laughed at anyone who said they believed in werewolves. Now he found himself wondering just how many people knew the true situation. He and Kate had been directed here to find Jicaque, but it was feeling more and more like they had been lured into the secret werewolf capital of America.

"Stacy's gonna find a cure for the 'wolves," piped up Rico. "Make them just people again."

"She is?" Tom looked at him, then at Woollard, a jolt of fresh hope slamming through his heart. Maybe he wouldn't need to find their mystery medicine man; maybe a cure was closer than he could've dared hope. "Well?"

"That is the ultimate aim of her research, yes," Woollard confirmed. "But I fear there's a long way to go."

Tom felt a dizzying crunch of disappointment in his guts. "Right," he said, trying to act casual, aware that Jasmine was looking at him oddly. "How come you know so much about it?"

Woollard shrugged. "Obviously the study of werewolves is not her real work at the hospital. She can only appropriate so much hospital equipment to further her lupine researches." He tapped his scrawny chest. "So she's enlisted my expertise to aid her in her quest . . . and uses my private laboratory here when necessity dictates."

"Have you heard of a man called Jicaque?" Tom asked him.

"Never in my life," Woollard shot back. He cleared his throat. "Now, are you finished with your questions? Can I get back to Rico here, hmm?"

"Not yet," Tom replied, his anger rising at having his hopes dashed again so swiftly. "You were saying something about arranging for us to be picked up or delivered."

Woollard gave a bleak chuckle. "And I thought *I* had a persecution complex. I was referring to *these*." He reached behind him and pulled back the dull pink curtain that partitioned the room to reveal expensive-looking lab equipment ranged along the back wall, perched precariously on an antique desk. So much for the private laboratory.

He opened something that vaguely resembled a small refrigerator and revealed two miniature milk crates inside, both filled with stoppered test tubes. "Stacy requests, with some monotony, that I perform specialist treatments on certain lupine blood samples," he explained with a sigh. "We're working to perfect a very special serum. She gives me blood samples, I prepare an active solution of serum, she goes and gives it to her lupine patients, and I analyze the results."

"What is this serum?" Tom tried to keep the excitement from his voice. "A cure for turning 'wolf?"

Woollard shook his head. "More of a tonic. The

serum is intended to pacify lupine aggression." He smiled thinly. "I only wish I had one that worked on teenage aggression."

"Say you're sorry," Jasmine ordered Tom.

Tom felt the heat of her glare and felt himself blush. "Well, I'm . . . I'm sorry for barging in on you like that, Dr. Woollard."

"I'll *make* you sorry if you make me look a fool again," Jasmine muttered.

Woollard considered. "There *is* something you can do to make amends." He lifted the crates from the refrigerator, his shaking hands making the test tubes rattle alarmingly, and placed them in a secure metal chest stowed beneath the examination couch. "Dr. Stein said she needs these treated blood samples urgently—before she finishes her night shift over at Park East Hospital. She'd like to see Rico again, too."

"I bet she would," muttered Jasmine.

"I don't taste good to 'wolves," Rico piped up. "Stacy likes that."

"Anyway," Woollard went on. "If you'd undertake to deliver them to her right away, I'd be grateful."

"Sure," Tom said quickly. "I'd like to meet her." Maybe *she* had heard of Jicaque. And if she was working on a cure, maybe Tom's blood could help her out? Then he realized Jasmine was looking at him like he was a freak.

She turned to Woollard. "Are you sure it can't

wait, Doc?" she pleaded, rubbing her eyes. "It's getting kind of late for me."

"So I notice," said Woollard wryly. "But the trip will be worth your while. Dr. Stein has offered to give Rico free drugs for his asthma by way of reward."

Rico sighed. "Won't work."

Jasmine cuffed him lightly on the head. "They will if you take them regular, Rico!"

"Yeah, yeah," said Rico.

Woollard smiled bleakly as if at some private joke. "You're acting as though the remedy were worse than the disease, boy. That is, if I may misquote Bacon?" He scowled at the blank faces staring back at him. "Francis Bacon! You've surely heard of him?"

Tom hadn't. But at the mention of bacon, his stomach growled.

Woollard threw up his hands in despair. "Philistines. Where'd I leave my drink?" He wandered from the room, muttering to himself.

Jasmine turned to Tom. "Well," she said, "now that you've finished making us look totally stupid, why don't you carry that box back to our wheels so we can get the mercy run over with?"

Tom nodded. But he still wasn't totally convinced by Woollard. "Isn't it a little weird that he lives in a dump like this, but he's got all that high-tech equipment lying around?"

"It's his life," Jasmine replied shortly.

Tom wasn't sure if she meant it was Woollard's choice what he spent his money on or that high-end science stuff like that was what he lived for. As he hefted up the metal carrying case, he guessed she was right either way.

"Maybe we should go and find Kate," Tom ventured. "She could come with us."

"We take care of Rico first," Jasmine said.

"C'mon, Jas," Rico moaned. "I wanna get back and check Ramon."

"We will. Soon as Stacy's checked *you* out," Jasmine replied. "Ramon would want that."

Rico sighed and nodded, then led the way out. "Can't you take us there in a real *hot* motor, Jas?"

"You don't want to know how hot that Cadillac is going to be in a couple of hours when the cops start looking," she retorted, and then jerked her thumb at Tom. "And that's another good reason why we can't go cruising about town looking for his girl. But it'll get us to Park East okay. Then we ditch it for good."

Tom called a goodbye—Woollard didn't reply— and stepped out after them onto the dismal street. Rico shut the doctor's door, then skipped off after Jasmine. Tom had barely taken another step when he heard the bolts slide stiffly across, one after the other; the old doctor was back in hiding behind his locked doors and empty bottles.

Unable to shake his sense of unease, Tom stared about. There was no one around. The only moving object was a black Porsche, crawling away from him along the curbside, its engine barely breathing.

Still peering about warily, weighed down with the box of test tubes, Tom headed after Jasmine and Rico.

Jasmine drove carefully so as not to draw any unwelcome attention, picking a path that took them through the quieter streets. The dirty white of the New York dawn was slowly soaking through the sky. Soon another day would be under way and the wide-open streets would be clogged with the morning's traffic.

Rico was asleep in the back, despite the radio blaring. Jasmine kept switching stations, singing along with songs for a few lines, then tiring of them and hunting down others. The constant changing was starting to put Tom on edge. He was worried about Kate and exhausted by the craziness of the night.

Bored with the monotonous low-rise landscape, he looked at Jasmine instead. Man, she was pretty; her dark complexion flawless, the little stud in her snub nose glittering in the dawn light. Tom realized they'd been together for hours, yet he barely knew a thing about her. Maybe he could distract her from the station hopping with some dazzling conversation.

He nudged down the volume. "So, uh . . . How long have you been with Ramon?"

She glanced across at him. "I ain't *with* Ramon."

Tom felt flustered. "I . . . Well, I guess from what he said, I assumed . . ."

Jasmine yawned. "We went together for six months. Longest I've been with anyone. Something special at the time."

"What happened?" Tom asked.

She shrugged. "Life, I guess. I'm sixteen. I don't want to be tied down. He still got it for me, but we're just friends." She paused. "That the way with you and Kate?"

"Kind of."

Jasmine gave him a look out of the corner of her eye. "You two seemed pretty tight to me. You been with her, Tommy?"

The question hit straight and hard at some dark place deep inside him. There was no way he could even dream about that kind of relationship with Kate. It was out of the question while he remained 'wolf: It would bring about Kate's worst nightmare—her own lupine change—something she was determined would never happen. And besides, he didn't even know whether she was interested in him in that way. She seemed so much more sophisticated than he was.

He wished he hadn't started this conversation. And he felt a sudden, terrible shame that the creatures who now threatened Jasmine and her friends counted him among their number. If Jasmine knew his secret, would she scream right now?

"I'm taking this silence as a mad big yes, Tommy. You been with her."

"No," he said quietly. "We're just friends."

"For real?" Jasmine looked at him oddly.

"For real."

"Well, no skin off my ass." Jasmine clicked her tongue. "But are you sure *she* knows that?"

Tom felt a tingle travel over his skin, but before he could ask Jasmine what the hell she was talking about, a black Porsche came screaming out of a side street, turned, and came up fast behind them.

It was the car he'd seen outside Woollard's place. The low, sleek automobile could barely contain the thugs it carried, five of them in all, jostling around inside.

The Porsche surged forward and smashed into the back of the Cadillac. Rico was thrown forward against the back of the driver's seat.

"Seat belt!" Tom yelled at Rico, then turned to Jasmine. "Who are they? You know them?"

"Swagger's gang," she replied, trying to accelerate away.

But they couldn't hope to outrun the Porsche. "Hold on," Jasmine shouted as she swung the Cadillac around a corner so fast that Tom's head cracked against the window.

"*A cuánta velocidad puede ir esta máquina?*" Rico yelled.

Jasmine gritted her teeth. "I'm making it go as fast as I can, okay?"

But in seconds the Porsche was back on their tail. Two of the passengers were hanging out the rear windows, waving, trying to get them to pull over.

"Bite me," Jasmine muttered, and floored the Cadillac.

The lights ahead were green, but there was a line of three or four cars ahead of her. Jasmine swung wide out and went careening past them through the intersection. Rico whooped in excitement in the backseat, gripping his seat belt with both hands. Drivers coming the other way jammed on brakes and horns together and swerved all around her as she sped through the cars like a sickle cutting a swathe through corn.

But the Porsche, faster and more maneuverable, was still on their tail, gaining on them.

"What do they want?" Tom shouted.

Jasmine tore around another corner. "I don't think it's to ask us to the prom." She cursed, eyeing the black car worriedly in the rearview mirror.

She was so distracted that it was Rico who first saw the garbage truck crawling out from an alley into the street ahead of them. "Jas!" he screamed.

There was no way they could steer past it and no way they could miss it at the speed they were traveling. Jasmine jerked up hard on the emergency brake—too hard. The rear wheels locked and the Cadillac was suddenly spinning around, out of control. The car mounted the curb, then smacked into a fire hydrant.

Tom felt his heart and stomach swap places as his body seemed to go into free fall. The world outside whizzed past, a blur of brick and metal—then asphalt and sky as the car tumbled over onto its back and scraped across the sidewalk. Woollard's carrying case clunked around in the trunk like a metal beast desperate for release, pounding as hard and loud as the blood in Tom's temples.

After long, screeching seconds they crashed into something and finally rocked to a halt. Tom gasped, choking for breath, suspended upside down by his seat belt. "Jasmine," he gasped. He could smell smoke, could hear the fizzing of the car's electronics shorting. "Jasmine?"

She stirred and groaned. She had a cut on her forehead, but she was alive, thank God.

"Rico? You okay?" she asked, her voice slurring a little.

"Ayudame," Rico said softly, his eyes tightly shut. *"Ayuda."*

Even Tom knew that meant "help." As he fought to unbuckle his seat belt, he could hear anxious voices shouting—the garbagemen, he guessed. And then he heard other voices, laughing and jeering. Coming toward them.

The anxious voices outside grew suddenly indignant, then angry. Tom heard punches and mocking laughter. Suddenly he gasped as the bloodied face of one of the garbagemen slammed into the passenger window beside him.

A second later someone else crouched down beside the window and peered in at Tom, smirking triumphantly. A trail of yellow shot through the man's dark eyes.

Tom's senses grew sharper, stinging his mind into focus. He felt the now-familiar ache and compulsion, the one that terrified and exhilarated him all at once. But he couldn't risk the transformation with Jasmine and Rico so close by.

Could he?

The smoke in the car grew thicker, beginning to screen out the leering lupine face at the window. "Jasmine, Rico! Wake up!" Tom yelled, still fumbling with the buckle on the seat belt. "We've got to get out of here!"

Jasmine turned her head to face him, her straight black hair hanging down, brushing against the pale roof fabric. "What's happening?" she murmured.

"I can smell gasoline." Tom pried desperately at the stubborn buckle. "I think the car's going to explode or something."

The car rocked again as someone slammed up against it. Tom couldn't see who; the smoke was too thick now.

Jasmine stared about, wide-eyed. "Is that the cavalry?"

"Cavalry getting their asses kicked," Tom said. His insides felt on fire. The urge was becoming overwhelming. It would be so easy. . . . "No!" he yelled in frustration. "Come on! Open!" He gasped with effort as he put all his strength into forcing open the stuck buckle. "Come *on!*"

But his human strength wasn't enough. He was still trapped, powerless to get Jasmine and Rico out of there. His blood burned hot in his body, his mouth stung with the tang of iron. The 'wolves from the Porsche could break in and do *anything* to them while he and Jasmine and Rico just hung there, helpless. . . .

And then, though his head was swimming, Tom heard the quiet whoosh of flames igniting. He gave in to the change at last.

As he roared at the delicious pain coursing through his body, the windshield shattered. Arms reached in through the smoke that belched out from the fusing elements in the dashboard, fingers urgently groping the air, searching them out.

Chapter Seven

"No! Leave us alone!"

To Tom, with his heightened hearing, Jasmine's shriek was almost deafening. Flames were now licking at the window beside him. As his clothes tore open, as his bones warped and his body refashioned itself into sleek lupine form, Tom fought to retain control, to stop himself from simply tearing into their attackers. He had to focus on getting Jasmine and Rico safely out before the whole car went up. Only that mattered.

But the smoke was being sucked out through the jagged hole in the windshield, and the air was clearing. He was exposed.

"Jesus, you're one of them!" Jasmine screamed, tears rolling down her face.

The seat belt could no longer support Tom's bulk. The fabric snapped and he fell against the roof of the car. One of the groping hands fastened around his throat and he snapped at it, drew tangy blood, began to drool.

Jasmine writhed in her seat, still dangling upside down, trying to free herself from the belt. "Keep away from me!" she yelled—at Tom, at the groping hands, at the flames that were now roaring up beside the driver's side window.

A loud clunk from the rear of the car sent a sudden realization sparking through Tom's clouded thoughts. The hands hadn't been reaching in for them at all. They'd been searching for the switch on the dash that opened the trunk.

The thugs in the Porsche didn't give a damn about Jasmine or Rico or Tom. They wanted the test tubes of blood from Woollard's apartment, chilled and packed tight in that frosty metal box. Tom didn't know why, and right now he didn't much care. He only wanted to fight back.

With their objective achieved, the hands withdrew. The car began to rock up and down as the heavies attempted to raise the burning car enough to open the trunk lid and pry out the gory hoard inside.

Tom nuzzled his lupine head into Jasmine's waist. She yelled and pummeled his skull with her fists, but he barely felt the blows. Her musky cologne irritated his sensitive nose, masked the smell of her flesh. . . . His teeth scraped against the skin of her stomach. He drooled over her and she shrieked. If he bit her, she would stop. If he bit her, he could feed. . . .

No! He tore his head away from her, tugging

through the fabric of her seat belt as he did so. It snapped, and she fell half on top of him. She recoiled, pushing against him, kicking him as she struggled to get clear.

"It's okay, Jas!" Rico shouted to her above the din. "It's okay. It's still Tom!"

Jasmine froze and stared into Tom's eyes. Her own were streaming from the smoke and the terror, but she didn't blink or break contact. Then slowly, trying not to shake, she nodded.

Rico had wriggled free of his own belt and was staring at Tom in wonder. Past him, through the rear windshield, Tom saw the Porsche 'wolves dragging Woollard's metal carrying case clear of the car. His eyes narrowed in fury at the thought of all they had done.

He turned to the front and punched at the remaining shards of glass sticking out like teeth from the frame of the windshield. Then he grabbed the neck of Rico's shirt, hauling the boy clear of the blazing car.

As they emerged, Tom saw the garbage collectors lying beaten and dazed all around their vehicle, where the thugs had cleared them away from their prey. He could hear the slow, whining approach of distant sirens. Laying Rico on the ground, Tom turned to find that Jasmine had already crawled out by herself.

The thugs were clambering into the Porsche with their prize. Rage growled in Tom's belly. He bounded up onto the toppled car and flew at them.

He landed barely a yard from the battered sports car, but it was already going in reverse. One of the thugs had been left behind. He swung around to face Tom, swiping at him with a metal bar. The bar caught Tom heavily behind the ear, knocking him flat on the asphalt. Everything went hazy.

As the world rolled back into focus, Tom heard the engine of the Porsche receding into the distance. The thug who'd jumped him was scrambling away down a side street.

There was a deafening explosion as the Cadillac erupted in flames. The force of the blast sent Tom tumbling farther out into the street. Then he heard slight footsteps, someone running toward him. He tried to move, but his limbs were sluggish. He turned his head, bared his dagger teeth in warning. It was Rico, staring at him with his big, dark eyes.

"Stay away from him, Rico!" Jasmine warned. She was peering around from behind the garbage truck. It must have shielded her and Rico from the blast.

"He's hurt," Rico shouted back. "We got to get him out of here. He got *us* out."

Tom's 'wolf limbs were cramping up; his whole body was shaking. With the rage literally knocked out of him, he could feel his body preparing to shift back to human form. He would be weak, defenseless, exposed—not to mention stark naked. This place would be swarming with emergency services and crowds of onlookers anytime now. He couldn't be found here.

Rising jerkily to his feet, he limped toward the same side street the thug had taken, then paused and looked back. Jasmine had skirted the burning wreck and stood beside Rico, grabbing hold of his shoulders.

But Rico wriggled clear. "I think he wants us to go with him."

"What, so he's Lassie now?" Jasmine retorted. "Rico, he's a 'wolf. You know what they can do. You more than most."

"He's not like them, Jas, I swear it."

Tom ran for the side street, felt his teeth ache and his jaw tighten, felt his bones start to burn and melt as the metamorphosis took hold.

Time and motion blurred, and suddenly he was moving on two legs, not four, and he was freezing cold, slumped naked against a wall with his head thumping to the erratic beat of his heart. He felt for the wound from the iron bar. The speeding of his blood through the metamorphosis had reduced the damage to little more than an egg-shaped bump.

He turned to find Rico and Jasmine standing before him.

Jasmine's eyes had dried; she stood cold and composed. "Things ain't bad enough already? I got to see you butt naked now before I even get breakfast?" She held out a bundle of clothes—a fluorescent garbage collector's jacket, grimy trousers, and heavy boots. "Get these on."

Rico led them into a nearby vacant lot so that they were off the street, and Tom gratefully slipped on the baggy trousers. "Nice. I always wanted to be a garbageman."

"Figured you needed the clothes more than he did," Jasmine muttered. "Ambulance is coming for him now."

Rico smiled. "Jas can strip a guy faster than any girl I seen."

"Shut your mouth," she retorted, and looked back at Tom. "No wonder you wanted to go see Stacy Stein. You need the cure, don't you?"

"Yeah," Tom replied quietly.

"So, what—you going to stay this way now?"

"The urge to change happens when I get mad," Tom explained. "Or scared. Or when the moon's full."

Jasmine nodded, blew out a long sigh. "Rico's right. I guess you did help us. I was thinking maybe you were a spy, but now . . ."

"I'm not a spy. I helped Ramon too. That's how we met, in Central Park. He didn't want to tell you in case you freaked." Tom could see the doubt in her deep brown eyes. "Jasmine, everything Kate and I told you back at Ramon's was true. I'm no ordinary 'wolf. Takapa wants me for study, and Marcie Folan—Kate's mom—wants me dead."

"That bitch on TV," Jasmine recalled. "You say she's going to kill your folks if you don't give yourself up?"

"You're a wanted man," said Rico, his eyes shining like this was just some way cool game. "So what are you going to do?"

"I figure I've got maybe a day or so before Marcie moves again," he said, tying his borrowed boots. "There's supposed to be a man in this city who can cure me, but I don't know how to find him."

"That *Zhee-khaki* guy you asked Woollard about, right?" Jasmine nodded. "And you think maybe Stacy Stein knows?"

"If Stacy knows about the 'wolves and is researching a cure herself . . ." He shrugged. "It's the only lead I have."

Tom tested out the boots. They were at least two sizes too big but better than nothing. "You know, those 'wolves went to a lot of risk and trouble to get those test tubes of blood." He smoothed a hand through his tangled hair. "Why would they? Just what is this treatment Woollard's given the stuff?"

Jasmine shrugged. "Go ask him. Or Stacy."

"Hold on," Tom said, thinking. "Woollard said she needed them urgently. If I can get them back, she'll owe me a favor, right?" He looked at Jasmine and Rico. "The guy who slugged me went this way. I think I can pick up his scent; we can follow him."

Jasmine stared at him uncertainly. "You can do that when you're not howling?"

"Kind of. If I really concentrate."

"Tom, you're freaking me—"

"Quiet, Jas!" Rico slapped her arm. "Let the man concentrate!"

Trying to hide a wry smile, Tom led the way back onto the street and scented the air. The search was on.

Kate was beginning to wonder if she'd ever find a chance to escape. Swagger was sticking to her like glue, and while he'd mentioned bed a couple of times, she was quite sure sleep was not on his mind.

So far he seemed to find her reticence somehow cute. She just prayed he didn't tire of it too quickly. She guessed Swagger was used to getting his own way and probably enjoyed the use of force. Truthfully, she was scared stiff.

While Eric cleaned up the bloody arena, Swagger had announced he would give Kate a tour of his headquarters. She had the awful feeling that the tour would conclude in whatever stinking pit he used for a bedroom, and she knew she had to get away before then. But Shaun, his big bruiser body-guard, was keeping careful pace close behind and every door in the place was locked and bolted. Even if she ran, there was no way out.

Having walked her around the stadium and

shown her his video games room—a sort of squalid shrine to all things Xbox—they'd moved on to the main lobby. Kate was eyeing the boarded-up doors longingly when one of them started to thud and rattle.

Swagger grinned wide. "My boys are home." He gestured to Shaun. "Open up."

Shaun obeyed in silence, unbolting the doors.

"Your boys?" Kate queried, heart sinking.

"My generals," said Swagger. "We rule this city—it's just that the city don't know it yet. But it will."

"So," Kate deduced as Shaun threw the final bolts, "they've been checking out the other gangs in New York, making sure they'll all be at your big fight come Friday?"

Swagger's eyes were cold, his smile a little less sure on his face. "Clever kid. Yeah, we're through with the heats. Time now for the main event."

The doors were opened and four men burst in, all in almost drunken good spirits. They were Swagger clones: all grease, black leather, and denim. The tallest of them was hefting a metal carrying case. Swagger and Shaun greeted them with whoops and weird tribal salutes.

"You want a progress report, Swag?" said a barrel-chested man with a whiny voice, whose chest hair curled up to his pointed chin.

"Later, Mikey. When I ain't got company."

The tall guy looked at Kate and licked his lips. "See you got yourself breakfast already."

Swagger nodded and slapped Kate's butt. "And damn, am I hungry this morning."

Kate gritted her teeth.

"So, what's with the new purse, Kes?" Swagger demanded.

"Hope you're thirsty as well as hungry," said Kes, the tall guy. "'Cause we brought back a treat." He opened up the case and pulled out a test tube. A thick, dark syrupy liquid sloshed inside. Blood.

Swagger's face darkened. "What were you even thinkin' about, taking this?"

Mikey shrugged. "We can handle it, Swag."

Kes looked suddenly uncomfortable. "Thought we'd have a party to celebrate Friday night coming."

"You got no orders to!" Swagger advanced threateningly on his so-called generals. "Where'd you get this? And where's Danno?"

Mikey looked at the others for support. "We saw some of Ramon's gang taking it from Woollard's place. . . ."

"And you couldn't help yourselves, huh?" Swagger bore down on him, imitated Mikey's nasal Bronx accent. "*We can handle it, Swag!* Come on, what happened?"

Kate listened in horror as Kes and his buddies told Swagger about how they'd run a car off the road, and how the guy inside had turned 'wolf, and how Danno had slugged him with an iron bar while the rest of them took off. Danno was still out there somewhere, but the 'wolf wouldn't be going anywhere fast. . . .

They could only be talking about Tom and Jasmine. Exhausted, frightened now for Tom as much as for herself, Kate felt tears prickling the backs of her eyes. But she kept them inside. There was no way these animals would ever see her cry.

"You dumbass," Swagger told Kes, suddenly dead serious. "These tubes were meant for Stacy Stein over at Park East Hospital. She needs 'em, man!"

"*We* need 'em," said Mikey, and the others agreed.

Kes offered a tube to Swagger. "Hey, there's two crates of these babies. We can just take some, and—"

"You're no better that that scum in the locker room!" Swagger snatched the test tube away and smacked Kes in the face with enough force to floor him. "You don't do anything like this again, none of you, you hear?" he raged. "I'm ruling here. *Me*." He stabbed his grimy finger into Mikey's shoulder. "*I* say when you pull this kind of crap, and when I tell you to do something straight, you do it. Get me?"

Kes got up, wiped blood from his lip, and nodded silently. The others signaled their understanding too, the joking around all over, eyes downcast now.

But Kate realized that Shaun hadn't reacted to a single word or gesture. All his attention was on the test tube of blood in Swagger's hand. He was practically drooling, picking at his fingers and shuffling his feet around like he needed the bathroom.

Swagger noticed too. He selected another tube from the crate and handed it to Shaun. "I guess a little treat from time to time don't hurt."

Kate grimaced as Shaun pulled out the cork and held it to his mouth, about to drain it, but Swagger shook his head.

"Bad manners, man," he said. "First we drink a toast . . . to Dr. Stacy Stein, the dumbest bitch on the East Coast!"

He raised his tube mockingly to the others, then he and Shaun drank. Kes and the others eyed Shaun balefully now as the sticky red liquid disappeared down his throat. He shuddered and moaned softly as the last of it slipped down. Then he cracked open the glass tube and flicked his tongue over the slivers, determined not to miss a drop.

Kate had never seen any 'wolf get anything like this kick from blood in a tube. It was alien to the whole lupine culture. Their fix was the hunt, the felling of the prey, the opening of veins with scissoring jaws, the tearing of flesh—not just swigging blood from a glass like soda. She jumped as Swagger threw his own empty tube down at Kes's feet.

"You take the rest over to Park East right now," he commanded. "And no more dumb stunts, okay?" Then he turned and grabbed hold of Kate's hand so hard it hurt. "Come on, baby. No more games." His gray eyes were glassy, and he was squinting like he wasn't quite able to focus. "It's past time I saw a little more of you."

She tried to pull away, but his grip was too strong; he only laughed.

"What's the matter, sugar? Don't you want to have some fun?"

Kate wanted to puke in his face. "Sure, I do," she whispered, trying to keep herself from shaking, "I just want to go somewhere more private, you know?"

Swagger nodded, a slow smile of understanding spreading over his ugly face. "Chicks," he said, giving his generals a long-suffering look. "Okay. Come on."

He dragged her up three flights of crumbling stairs. "Where are we going?" she demanded.

"My office," he said, his words slurring a little now. "You're going to take some dictation, baby."

Kate found herself hauled into a fetid, airless dump of a room overlooking the arena. The walls were plastered with posters of bikes and airbrushed bikini bimbos, and the table was stacked high with stereo components and computer games. In the corner was a pile of guns, bats, and just about anything you could classify as an offensive weapon.

Swagger crouched over a CD player and stabbed at the buttons until a blast of thrash metal spewed out of a huge pair of speakers. "To get us in the mood," he said hoarsely, turning to face her.

Kate was beginning to feel nauseous. She tried to

curl her lips into what she hoped was a seductive smile. "Listen, do you have a bathroom? I need to freshen up."

He took a step closer, his bulk massive and threatening. "You smell good to me."

She batted her eyelids. "Pretty please?"

"Down the hall," he said, gesturing to the right. "Don't be long." He gave her a gruesome smile. "Or else I'll come find you."

"I'll come right back, sugar," she said, all doe-eyed. "And I don't want to see so many clothes on you when I do."

Swagger guffawed, leaned down, and placed a slobbery kiss on her neck.

Kate felt almost giddy. He actually believed she wanted him. He'd bought it—and she'd bought herself time. As he turned back to his stereo and started fiddling with the graphic equalizer, she discreetly lifted a metal crowbar from his pile of weapons and backed out of the office.

Once alone in the corridor she ran for the bathroom. As she threw open the door, she almost heaved—the air was rank, and the floor was wet with puddles of God knew what. The toilets were cracked and filthy, most of the doors hanging off their hinges. The bulk of the grimy tiles had long since crumbled away from the damp walls.

And the windows had been boarded up and barred.

Keeping calm, Kate grabbed a slimy wooden mop from the wet floor. Swiftly she rammed the shaft through the metal D of the door handle and pushed the end of it behind a chipped washbasin. Now the door was jammed. It might buy her a little time.

She ran over to the nearest window. Thankfully the sound of Swagger's music covered the sound of splitting wood as she used the crowbar to lever off a panel and smash through the dirty glass so she could see outside.

She swore. The bathroom overlooked the street and safety—but the only way out was a sheer drop down at least three stories.

"Kate?" There was a loud banging on the door. "Come on, who takes five minutes to use the bathroom?"

"I—I'm nearly through!" she shouted.

"Hey, the door's jammed. What you doing in there?"

"I . . ." She wished she knew. "I'll be two minutes. It's not like I can get out, right?"

Right.

But Swagger was bored with waiting. He was coming in whether she was ready or not.

CHAPTER EIGHT

Kate locked the cubicle door behind her; then she stood on the toilet to reach the small window. She began prying off one of the bars with the crowbar—she'd sooner jump than let Swagger get his filthy hands on her.

Swagger was still banging at the door. She put all her strength into levering off the bar. Finally it fell with a clang onto the floor.

"Hey, what was that? Open up!" Swagger started kicking and shoving at the door with greater force. With a scream of fury he finally broke inside. "Trying to split on me, huh? Think I'm stupid?"

Kate said nothing, concentrated on scraping the crowbar around the frame to clear the jagged splinters of glass remaining. But she gasped as the door behind her jumped and rattled under some great impact.

"I'm going to teach you," he bellowed, his voice wild and cracked with rage. "You don't mess with Swagger!"

She leaned out of the window, and the ground swam dizzily far below her. The door shuddered as

Swagger ran at it again, the bolt nearly snapping clean through. She looked above her this time—maybe she could climb to the next floor up. No, there was nothing, nothing but—

A half-rusted drainpipe ran to the right of the window.

It was suicide. But so was staying in here.

She heard Swagger breathing hoarsely. Either he was still in the mood or—

Uh-oh. Now she could hear bones clicking and popping and the first guttural stirrings of the lupine creature inside Swagger.

"'Wolf's at your door, baby," she heard him rasp.

Kate dropped the crowbar and desperately swung herself out through the window feet first. Clinging to the top of the window frame, balancing on the sill, she stretched out her long legs toward the rusting drainpipe. Edging forward till she teetered on the ledge, she could just grip the drainpipe with both ankles.

With a chilling roar Swagger smashed down the door at last. She caught a glimpse of matted fur, vivid yellow eyes, sharp teeth snapping for her. Then, her ankles still locked around the drainpipe, she twisted her body around and pushed away from the windowsill with both hands.

For a sickening second she was sure she would fall. Then, to her amazement, her outstretched palms were slithering over the rusting metal of the drainpipe.

Swagger's huge head burst through the window,

swinging around to face her, snarling and snapping at her. But the window was too small for him to lean out any farther. He howled in impotent rage.

Kate began to shinny down. The pipe was cold as she gripped it with both hands, the brackets that held it to the wall rusted and weak. Her lifeline began to creak ominously. She winced in pain as metal fragments stuck in her palms, and tried to slide down as smoothly as she could. Then the section of pipe she was clinging to pulled away from the wall. Kate was so horrified she couldn't even cry out. The world whistled about her as she fell, arms and legs flailing.

Her fall was broken by a couple of trash cans that—thank God—couldn't have been emptied for weeks. They were filled to overflowing with bags of soft, slimy garbage that worked like smelly air bags. Her landing was painful and humiliating instead of fatal.

"Would you mind getting out of there? You're making the trash all dirty."

Kate looked around wildly and saw a dark figure looming over her. It was a garbage collector. Where had he sprung from? Why was he grinning like a—?

"Tom!" she wailed in disbelief.

He helped her up. "Next time you escape from somewhere, why not try the stairs?" He sounded cool and casual, but the light in his eyes told her how pleased he was to see her. He pointed up at Swagger, still framed in the window. Thick drool was stringing down from the 'wolf's slavering jaws. "I guess we should get out of here, huh?"

"Right now," she muttered. She took a few tentative steps—her legs felt bruised and wobbly, but at least they weren't broken—then turned and gave Swagger the finger. "I said you wouldn't believe what I'd do to you," she shouted, "you sick, evil bastard."

The beast stared down at Kate. Then abruptly it vanished from the window.

Tom took her hand as she hobbled over to the corner of the half-derelict building. Jasmine and Rico were waiting there.

"You were right, Tom," said Rico, grinning from ear to ear. "She was in there!"

"Let's move," said Jasmine, and started to sprint away down the street. The others set off after her.

Kate noticed Rico was wheezing. "Is he okay?"

"Not really," Tom muttered.

"He'll be fine," Jasmine said hotly, skittering to a stop. "Rico, get on my back."

"I can carry him," Tom protested as Rico dutifully climbed aboard.

"No," she said, "I got him."

With Rico clinging on around her neck, she moved off again—but at least now at a speed Kate and Tom could better match.

"I thought you were dead," Kate said.

"So did I," Tom answered. "A couple of times."

"How the hell did you find me at that place?" she

panted, gesturing to his outfit. "Were you emptying their trash or something?"

"Funny. But don't think this uniform means I have to take any garbage from you!" He gave her a smile. "We followed the trail of some 'wolf who tried to kill us. Only when it led us to the arena, I could've sworn there was a scent of you about the place."

She frowned at him. "You saying I smell?"

"I thought it was my imagination." He sniffed. "But now that you've taken a bath in the trash . . ."

She stuck out her tongue. "Believe me, there's worse garbage inside that place. You won't believe what those freaks are doing."

"Tell me later," Tom puffed. "God, Kate, is it ever good to see you."

"Sure, it is," she said, and put on an extra spurt of speed so he wouldn't see she was smiling.

Jasmine and Rico led them down narrow, deserted alleyways. Finally they emerged onto a busier avenue. Early risers were already trailing up and down the sidewalks, shopkeepers were rolling up steel gates, and warm, steamy smells wafted out of bakeries.

Jasmine finally called a halt and crouched down so a reluctant Rico could clamber off her back. "Too many people around here for them to try something," she said, acting like she'd barely broken a sweat. "Y'all wait here. I'll fix us some wheels and we can get back to Ramon's."

Rico nodded approval, but Tom seemed less

certain. "Stealing two cars in one morning? Isn't that pushing your luck?"

"You think we've been lucky so far today?" She shook her head, apparently amused, and gave Tom's ass a playful swat as she passed by. "Be ready, people."

Kate stared in astonishment at Jasmine's retreating figure, then folded her arms and regarded Tom. "I see you made a new friend." She doubted his red cheeks were entirely caused by running.

"We've been through some stuff, I guess," Tom said.

"That's the truth," said Rico brightly.

Kate mustered all her usual cool. "Well, while we wait for her to get back, why don't you tell me all about it?" she suggested, jutting out her chin. "All the juicy details." But it felt like there was some screwed-up ball of something sour deep inside her, a spiky feeling she couldn't swallow down. *God strike me dead,* she thought. *All this crap going down and I get jealous for the first time in my life.*

"Hey," said Rico, pointing to a newsstand in delight. "You two are famous outlaws again. Cool! You should get out of sight, fast."

Kate read the headline screaming off the paper: TERROR TEEN COUPLE SIGHTED IN NEW YORK. "*Cool's* one word for it," she muttered.

Jasmine found them a battered station wagon. "What did you expect?" she told the disappointed Rico. "This ain't Park Avenue."

They all caught up on the car journey back to Ramon's hangout. Tom could hardly believe Kate's story—his own adventures seemed like nothing next to her ordeal. Maybe she blamed him on some level for running out on her? There was a coldness about her now, a distance—but maybe she just needed some time.

They spent the last minutes of the journey in silence. Tom shivered as he recognized the slum tenement they'd half dragged, half carried Ramon to last night. The door gaped open, hanging on a hinge. People walked by like it was nothing, like they hadn't noticed a thing.

"Ro?" called Rico, first out of the car and scampering up the steps to the ruined kitchen area. "Ro, you there? *Estas bien?*"

"Rico!" came Ramon's raw voice from somewhere inside the place.

"Thank God," murmured Jasmine, and ran after Rico.

Tom turned to Kate. "You sure you're okay?"

"Yes," she said. "Just thinking about Mom."

Tom grimaced. "With our pictures all over the *New York Post,* how long till we're seen and caught?"

Kate nodded. "She won't be leaving town till she's found us, that's for sure." She started to go after Jasmine and Rico.

"Wait." He took hold of her arm. "Do you think your mom will really kill my folks?"

Kate looked at him. "I don't know, Tom," she answered quietly. "If she does kill them, she'll have no hold over you. But then, we know she's crazy. . . ."

Tom sighed. "If I could find a cure, we'd be free of this nightmare."

Kate nodded again. "We should get back to looking for Jicaque."

"Yeah, let's talk to Stacy Stein," Tom replied. "Woollard said her work on a cure has a long way to go, but she might have come across Jicaque through her research."

"Swagger told his minions to make sure Stacy got those samples back. But then he said she was the dumbest bitch on the East Coast," Kate said thoughtfully. "Why would he have said that?"

"No idea—but coming from him, that's a recommendation," Tom growled.

Kate smiled. "Okay, but if we do go see her, what's to stop her from calling the cops the second she sees us?"

"I'm cute as a button?" Tom suggested hopefully.

The light went out of Kate's face. "Well, some people seem to think so," she snapped, and marched inside.

They found Ramon in the wrecked TV room, sprawled on a cushion, clutching his brother tight, like a kid with a teddy bear. His olive complexion was waxy, crusty with blood. Polar was standing in the corner, shifting about nervously, his camera raised over his hooded face. He snapped his flash at Tom and Kate, and another square of paper spewed out from the camera.

Tom found his backpack discarded under a table and searched it for fresh clothes. No luck: he'd ripped through his last pair of jeans.

Jasmine was boiling some water and fussing around with the first aid box. "What are you even doing here, Ramon?" she grumbled. "You're hurt bad. You need Doc Woollard."

"Don't need no one," Ramon snapped back. "Don't *got* no one." He looked up at Tom and Kate over Rico's shoulder. "My people all cleared out. Puff got himself a bed at Mount Sinai—they'll know he's jumped parole, man! Cops gonna be all over his fat ass."

"Guess he was real scared, huh, Ramon?" said Rico.

"And Cicero skipped to New Jersey, bailing out with the rest. Only Polar stayed behind." He lowered his voice, shook his head. "Just me and the fool. Cozy, huh?"

"What's up, Ramon?" Jasmine dabbed several swabs of cotton in the hot water. "We're here. Girls and little kids don't count?"

Ramon glanced over at her. "Yeah, you do," he said quietly. He turned back to Tom and Kate. "Rico tells me you looked after him good, wolf boy. And Kate, you saved my ass from Swagger out there on the street. I owe you both."

"So how about you get yourself checked out by this Dr. Woollard?" Kate said. "I'd hate to think we saved your ass just so it could go septic."

"Okay." Ramon sighed heavily. Rico moved aside as Jasmine came back in and started swabbing at his injuries.

Tom raised his arms in his baggy fluorescent jacket. "And since I'm fresh out of clean shirts, if you have any spare clothes a little less conspicuous than these . . ."

"Got some gear in the sleep room," offered Ramon. He spoke through gritted teeth, wincing. "Help yourself to whatever ain't been burnt."

Tom screwed up his nose as he entered the gloomy room. It reeked of smoke and charred plastic. The fire had done some damage, but it hadn't consumed everything in the closet. He pulled out some combat boots and a black tracksuit top—nice and inconspicuous.

He got back to find Jasmine cleaning up Ramon's head.

Ramon winced as she dabbed antiseptic onto his sticky scalp. "Jas, you take Rico over to Park East to see Stacy," he ordered. "Me and Polar, we'll hit Woollard's." He looked up at Tom. "Guess you two'll be taking off now, huh?"

"Tom says he wants to meet Stacy," Jasmine broke in.

"We both do," added Kate quickly.

Jasmine shrugged. "Guess there's room in the wagon."

"And, uh . . . your cop radio's still working, right?" Tom asked haltingly, and Ramon nodded. "I was wondering if you'd mind listening in, just in case you hear anything about my parents? The police must be in touch with them."

"Okay, change of plan." Ramon turned to Polar: "You want to stay here and eavesdrop on New York's finest?"

Polar nodded, then slouched past them through to the room with the radio. He dragged out a chair and sat facing the squawking metal box, staring at it through the camera like it was about to scuttle off somewhere.

"So what you waiting for?" growled Ramon to the rest of them. "Get out of here."

"Later, Ramon," said Rico, bumping knuckles as the others added their farewells.

"That's right." Ramon smiled, mussed up Rico's hair with his palm. "See y'all later. *Cuídate.*"

Kate glanced back and smiled. "Keep safe yourself."

The smile faded from her face as she followed the others out into the cold sunlight onto the bare, unwelcoming street.

"Keep safe," Tom echoed softly, and the run-down world around him seemed to laugh in his face.

Chapter Nine

Tom and Kate hung back while Jasmine and Rico marched up to the admissions desk at the Park East Virology Unit. They took seats in the waiting room beside a woman slumped in her chair with a brown leather coat draped over her, softly snoring.

"Wish I could grab a few z's myself now," muttered Tom, rubbing his eyes. Kate nodded.

"Rico Carranza to see Dr. Stacy Stein," Jasmine announced to the desk clerk. "She's expecting him."

"That's right! I am!" cried the woman beside Tom, scaring him half to death. Jasmine and Rico spun around in surprise as the woman jumped up from the chair like it was electrified and stared at them, her ice blue eyes wide and bright. "Good to see you again, Rico. And Jasmine—you thought any more about trying to get yourself on that mentoring program?"

"Yeah, I thought about it," Jasmine replied curtly.

"Think about it some more. It'd be good for you." Dr. Stein enjoyed a noisy, extravagant stretch, bending her body backward. "I've been waiting for you out here since my shift ended—must've fallen asleep. I guessed you'd wandered off somewhere when I collected the package from reception."

Now it was Tom's turn to jump up. "Those blood samples from Dr. Woollard?"

Dr. Stein turned to face him. She was probably in her early thirties, her features well defined and framed by coppery, shoulder-length hair. "You know about those?" she asked, not accusingly, just interested.

Tom lowered his voice. "And about the 'wolves, Dr. Stein," he confirmed.

She didn't seem particularly surprised. "Call me Stacy," she said, but as she held out a hand in greeting, she peered at him closely. "Your face looks familiar."

Please don't let there be a newspaper around here, Tom thought, returning her strong handshake. "Just one of those faces, I guess. I'm Tom. I was with Jasmine and—"

"Wait, wait." Stacy shook her head, her voice falling to a whisper. "Not with all these people around. Besides, this sounds like a long story and long stories are always better with coffee and bagels." She held out her hand to Kate. "Am I right, Miss . . . ?"

"Kate," she said, shaking the outstretched hand. "And I think you're the rightest person I ever met."

Stacy led them to a coffee shop deep inside the hospital and ordered for everyone before bustling over to a hexagonal table. "Sit down, all," she said, drumming her fingers on the tabletop until they were seated, "and let's get the introductions out of the way."

Tom and Kate told their separate stories over plastic foam cups of burned-tasting coffee while Rico and Jasmine filled their faces with bagels and cream cheese. Tom detailed the chase for the blood samples and the risks Swagger's men took to get them, and Kate confirmed how Swagger himself arranged for what was left to reach Stacy.

Stacy gave a low whistle. "Weird goings-on, all right."

"It *was* weird," Kate said. "Swagger was furious with the thugs who'd stolen the samples. He said you needed them."

"I do; they're very valuable to my work." Stacy seemed strangely moved. "For a lupine to have said that—he must be counting on me coming through for them."

"Uh . . ." Kate paused awkwardly. "Actually, he called you the dumbest person on the East Coast."

Stacy shrugged. "I'm not in this line of work for the applause," she said mildly. "Oh, those poor kids . . ."

"Excuse me?" Tom frowned at her. "Those poor kids are maniacs."

"Murderers," Kate added.

Jasmine agreed. "Did you miss the part where they almost killed *us* to get that stuff?"

"I'm sorry," said Stacy. "Of course it's wrong,

what they did. But it's not entirely their fault. They're lupine now, desperate for anything that'll help them cope with the newfound needs, with the conflicts that being 'wolf entails."

"So am I," Tom blurted, and immediately regretted it.

Stacy stared at him. "*You're* lupine?"

"He's a newblood," Kate said quietly, "not long turned."

"And I hate it," Tom said. "When I was first bitten, I fought; I was able to resist the change—like Rico."

Jasmine nodded. "Rico got bitten, but he didn't change."

Tom scowled. "But unlike Rico, I was bitten, locked up for a month, and force-fed turning herbs and potions."

"By my mother," Kate put in bitterly. "Finally he couldn't resist anymore."

"But Tom ain't like the other howlers," chirped Rico, chewing on a big bite of bagel. "He ain't mean and hungry; he don't chase people down. He saved us! And he keeps his own eyes."

"Tom retains some human control when in the lupine form," Kate explained. She paused. "We think he's a wereling."

"Wereling, huh?" Stacy looked at Tom coolly. "And maybe a killer too, right?" She turned to Kate. "With your accomplice here. I just figured out where I'd seen you before. The TV news on my break last night."

Tom met her stare. "It's not what you think, I promise."

Stacy raised her eyebrows. "I don't know. I guess I'm supposed to turn you in."

"No!" Rico cried, "you can't!"

Jasmine looked set to speak up too until Stacy waved them all into silence. "I won't. Selfish, I guess—but whatever you've done, I want to run some tests on you, Tom. If your story's true, I think you could be a lot of help to me."

"It *is* true," he said vehemently, "and I'll help you in any way I can."

Stacy smiled and nodded. "And you know, maybe I can help you. Kate, those long black tresses of yours are gorgeous, sure—but just a little distinctive for a girl on the run, don't you think?"

"I never really thought . . ." Kate put a hand to her hair. "What, you think I should chop it all off?"

"And you could give it to Tom to wear, like a wig," suggested Rico unhelpfully.

Stacy waved a dismissive hand. "Oh, he's just your average guy. Who'd look at him twice?"

"Gee, thanks," Tom said.

"Anyway, believe it or not, guys"—Stacy straggled her fingers through her own coppery hair—"this isn't natural. I've got some henna in my locker. Kate, you're welcome to try some."

Kate shrugged. "If you think it will help."

"It'll help *me* feel happier if I'm caught helping

wanted felons," said Stacy dryly. "Why, officer, this girl *can't* be that killer in the paper, not with that gorgeous red hair. . . ." She grew more serious. "Kate, is your whole family lupine?"

"Purebloods. Mom's from the Hargrave family line, Dad's a Folan," Kate said. "Two of the oldest families around."

"So you're a pureblood female, huh?" Stacy nodded to herself and chewed a bite of bagel thoughtfully. "All that lupine potential awaiting activation, wow . . . Doing it with a 'wolf presses the button— that's the way it works, right?"

Out of the corner of his eye Tom saw Jasmine perk up at that. He flushed and concentrated on his coffee cup.

Kate flinched. "Your bedside manner sucks."

"I'm sorry," said Stacy. "Really. That's tough for you."

Kate sipped her coffee. "Yeah."

"And for me too. I won't be able to learn much from your blood till your lupine cells are in gear. . . ."

Kate looked appalled at the thought. "Sorry," she said. "I'd rather die than let my lupine cells 'get in gear.' But believe me," she added, "my mother's trying to help you out." She wound a finger distractedly through her hair. "How about you? How come you're so interested in lupines?"

Stacy shrugged. "I'm a virologist. I study viruses and the diseases they cause. To me, lycanthropy—

the transformation into the lupine state—is just another infectious medical condition."

"A lot of people wouldn't see it that way," Tom pointed out. "These are *werewolves* we're talking about."

"I don't care for terms like *werewolf*." Stacy shook her head decisively. "People are so conditioned by all that cheap horror movie crap. If they ever found out the truth about lycanthropy—about how many real lupines operate in this city—there'd be wide-spread panic."

"Right," said Jasmine dryly. "When the poor folk are just hungry, the good people don't give a damn. But when the poor folk grow fangs . . . that's when the good people take notice."

Stacy passed her another bagel. "I know it's tough, but that's the situation we're dealing with. People can't handle the truth. That's why the work I'm doing isn't sanctioned or funded by the hospital authorities, why it has to stay completely unofficial. Just me and a few sympathetic health workers who turn a blind eye when they need to. We're working to do something about the situation before it gets completely out of hand."

"That's why you have to use people like Woollard," Tom concluded.

Stacy nodded. "Funding cutbacks at the hospital last year meant that I lost a lot of the equipment I'd come to depend on. So, yeah, I turned to Dr.

Woollard." Her tone softened. "Despite the booze, he's still a brilliant man. And he's really helped me out. With this kind of research I can't outsource sample preparation and testing to any regular lab. I really rely on him."

"You ever hear of a man called Jicaque?" Tom asked. "We came here to find him."

"The big-deal shaman guy, right?" Stacy replied. "Yeah, he got in touch once. He sent me some herbs that were meant to boost the body's defenses against cellular mutation. But it was so hard to run proper trials that I—"

Tom cut her off. "You've never seen him, met with him?"

"Never even talked to him," she admitted. "Sorry."

Tom shrugged defeatedly. "Forget it," he said. *And so should I.*

"But Stacy, how come *you* got involved with all this?" Kate persisted.

Stacy busied herself spreading cream cheese on another bagel. "My husband. He was a brilliant man, a top surgeon. Some lupine bitch in the meat-packing district wanted him for a mate, so one night he was turned." She gave a short, humorless laugh. "Maybe that's why lupines don't scare me. The dark mystique of a creature of legend kind of weakens when you have to wash his underpants each week."

"What happened?" Tom asked quietly.

"He stayed true to his vows—true to *me*—in spite of all she offered him. He hated what he'd become but was powerless to fight it." There was something hard in Stacy's eyes as she looked at Tom. "Unlike you, unlike Rico, he had no resistance. Oh, he tried, sure. . . . But in the end the 'wolf grew too strong."

Tom watched as she gouged doughy chunks from the bagel with her fingernails.

"I watched him suffer day after day. But I couldn't help him." She flashed a small and watery smile around the table. "He took his own life. So now I try to help the other victims of this . . . condition as best I can."

A heavy silence had fallen like a shroud over the table.

"I'm sorry, you did ask for a side order of sob story with your breakfast, didn't you?" Stacy joked. "Come on. Finish up and let's get to work. Rico, I'll write you a scrip for your asthma if you give me some blood, okay?"

He grimaced. "Some deal."

"And Tom," said Stacy, "I'd like to test some of your blood too, see how it compares. Kate, you want to do your hair while you're waiting?"

"I guess," said Kate doubtfully.

"I'll get you that henna. And some surgical gloves. Henna stains your skin if you're not careful, so gloves are a must. And plentiful around here."

"I wondered why you'd dye your hair in the hospital and not at home," Tom said.

Stacy smiled. "That's mainly because this place *is* my home, pretty much. I don't even remember the inside of my own bathroom." She paused. "Anyway, don't get me started. Hey, Jasmine, you going to help Kate with her hair?"

Jasmine and Kate looked at each other.

"Mmm, that sounds like fun," said Jasmine.

Kate scowled. "I can manage by myself, thanks."

Oh, brother, Tom thought.

"So what is it you're trying to achieve with your work?" Tom asked, watching the silver needle point slip under his skin.

Stacy gently eased out the plunger of the syringe, and it filled with his blood. "I'm working to isolate what I call the 'wolf factor'—the gene in lupine cells responsible for the metamorphosis. Once I've isolated it, I can work on a way of neutralizing it."

"You think that's possible?" Tom asked.

"I'm close, I'm sure of it." She swabbed at the tiny bead of blood left by the needle in the crook of his arm. "Thanks to Rico. His blood is special stuff: It contains a highly reactive enzyme that seems toxic to the lupine system."

Tom settled back on the examination table. "What does this enzyme do?"

"It attacks lycanthropic cells, causes fatal mutations

in the chromosomes." She poured the blood into a petri dish. "And since the lupine metabolism is far faster than a human's, the cellular degeneration occurs so fast that the immune system is swamped."

"So, translating," Tom ventured, "any 'wolf attempting to chow down on Rico might as well swallow rat poison. Right?"

"Right. I've been introducing Rico's blood to samples of both lupine and human blood and comparing the effects on the cells. If I can isolate all the genes affected in the lupine blood . . ."

"You'll have found werewolf DNA," concluded Tom. "Neat."

She tapped the petri dish. "Your blood could be a great help. Your resister gene should still be present even if it's been mutated by the 'wolf factor. By comparing your sample to Rico's, we can find out which genes you share. It should speed up the search."

"It's been slow work, huh?"

"Damn slow." Stacy sighed, pushing back her hair absentmindedly. "Even with a genius like Woollard helping me out."

Tom frowned. "I must be slow too. Why would the 'wolves go to all that trouble just to steal some blood samples?"

Stacy shook her head. "They weren't just blood samples, remember? Woollard treated them—turned them into Stacy serum."

"Into what?"

"The interim measure until I find a proper cure: Stacy serum." She smiled. "I believe that the cravings of the 'wolf—bloodlust, aggression, the urge to hunt—are just symptoms of the lupine infection."

"This is what Woollard was talking about," Tom realized. "The stuff in his case."

Stacy opened the lid of the case they'd taken from Woollard's and produced one of the test tubes filled with crimson liquid. "You've heard of certain synthetic drugs being used to treat heroin addiction?" she asked him. "This stuff's kind of similar. It's just blood but with a synthetically derived hormone mixed in—a hormone that simulates the kick lupines get from the 'wolf change and all it leads to."

"So . . . a consequence-free high?" Tom regarded the test tube doubtfully. "They sip that and the 'wolf cravings are satisfied? They lose their bloodlust?"

"I've tried it out on a number of subjects," she said. "The hospital's linked with a program run for homeless kids. Out on the streets, no place to go, they're easy pickings for the 'wolves. A lot of them were turned against their will and hate what they've become. So I put out the word—Stacy serum might just help them."

"And it really works?"

"According to my 'wolf informants on the program, the number of turns on the street has gone way down."

"Down?" Tom frowned. "But Ramon—Rico's

brother—was saying there are more 'wolves on the streets now than ever."

"Maybe it just seems that way to him," suggested Stacy. "I'm talking about the citywide picture. The evidence suggests there are fewer reports of fresh turnings and a greater number of newbloods coming back for more serum. The serum fixes the newbloods' cravings without them having to go out and bite someone. And because fewer people are being bitten, the 'wolf population explosion has slowed right down. The results add up."

"Okay," Tom said guardedly. "But if you can't make the stuff here, how are you meeting all this demand?"

"This is my starter pack for the latest brand of serum," Stacy explained. "It works like a vaccine. Just a few drops added to a beaker of blood plasma 'infects' it, turns it into *more* Stacy serum."

"And you have access to tons of plasma 'cause this is a hospital," Tom reasoned.

Stacy grinned. "Neat, huh?"

"And are there any side effects?"

"Nothing much has been reported, but I can't be completely sure. It's still work in progress, not perfected yet," she said a touch irritably. "But it's working all right for now. It's all we have, and it's offering the newbloods hope. Hope enough to hang on until I can perfect a cure."

"But Stacy—Kate saw Swagger take some of

your serum and it didn't exactly calm him down."

"Its actual effectiveness may vary in degree from case to case," Stacy said. "I'm working on that. Maybe that's why he made sure the rest of the shipment got back to me," she suggested. "Maybe he wants a serum that will work for *him*. He must realize he can't go out hunting the whole time without winding up in trouble eventually."

"I guess," Tom said, unconvinced.

She sighed. "You hate the 'wolves, Tom, I can understand that. But isn't it possible that's coloring your judgment? Making you *over*suspicious?"

Tom didn't want to push the point and risk pissing her off. "I want to believe you." He paused. "And I want to try some of the serum."

"I haven't checked your blood yet," said Stacy. "If there's less lupine in you than in the regular newbloods, the serum may be less effective."

"Consider me a guinea pig," Tom said. "I feel the blood cravings, Doctor, believe me. If there's a way to suppress that, I'll take it."

Stacy looked uncertain for a moment, then nodded. "Why don't you try to get some rest first, huh? You look dead on your feet, and it's going to take a while to do these tests on Rico." She smiled. "I'll fix you a dose of serum for when you wake up."

Tom yawned and nodded. "I guess it has been a long night."

●   ●   ●

Kate was catnapping on a hospital stretcher that seemed skinnier than she was; she was afraid even to turn over in case she fell out. Her head rustled every time she moved, since her hair was covered by a plastic bag. The henna stank, and she was dreading what she might see in the mirror when she was done.

Whatever—it had to be better than the stuff she was seeing in her restless dreams. Stacy had cordoned off a section in one of the wards so she could get a few hours' rest in private. But each time she dozed, she found herself back at the arena, Swagger's big, sweaty body beside her, the violence in the rink being reenacted again and again.

A cell phone rang close by and she sat up bolt upright. When the tinny melody clicked off, she heard Jasmine's voice answer, sleepy and irritable. She must've been getting some rest here too.

"Polar? Jesus, it's a miracle! He has a voice!"

Kate felt her stomach twist. Polar had been monitoring the radio—was he calling with news of Tom's parents?

"A guy? What guy? Say his name again? Zhee-khaki? Hey, I heard of him. . . ."

Kate was wide awake now. She jumped off her narrow bed, secured the bag over her hair, tried to follow Jasmine's voice. "Did he say Jicaque? Keep him on the line." She yanked aside a curtain and exposed a grouchy old woman getting a shot from a nervous-looking intern. "I'm sorry," she muttered, pulling it straight back across and moving on. "Jasmine! Let me talk to him."

She found Jasmine at last, a few cubicles down. As Kate watched, Jasmine killed the call with a precise press of her finger.

"Well, look at you." Jasmine smirked. "Bag on your head's a nice touch. No cop's going to recognize you now."

"Why'd you hang up?" Kate demanded. "Didn't you hear me?"

"Polar don't talk to people he don't know," Jasmine said, putting away the phone. "Fact is, Polar don't like to talk, period. His daddy beat him every time he opened his mouth, so pretty soon he learned—keep quiet and you keep out of trouble." She gave Kate a look. "He's choosy about who he talks to. So I took a message."

Kate crossed her arms. "Well?"

"Some old guy came around the hangout. The guy Tom's been looking for. Zhi—"

"Jicaque. Go on."

"He wanted to see Tom. Left instructions to meet on Gun Hill Bridge, out in Baychester. Nine o'clock tonight."

"That's it? Nothing else?"

Jasmine went sour faced. "What do you want, faxed confirmation and a map?"

Kate was seething with anger. "I just would've

liked to talk with him, okay? You don't have to be such a bitch."

Jasmine's eyes widened in outrage. "Me, the bitch?"

"Look, could you just call him back, please?" Kate took a deep breath. "You're right, Jicaque is the man Tom and I came to New York to see, but the 'wolves know that too. They could be using him to trap us or . . ."

Jasmine was shaking her head, looking around like she was bored.

Kate bunched her fists, feeling suddenly helpless. "*What* is your problem?"

"I'll tell you about my problem." Jasmine stood up and jabbed a finger into Kate's chest. "I don't want you talking to my friends, okay? We got enough problems. Something must've freaked Polar pretty bad to get him talking—and I don't want the people I care about mixed up in your crap the way Tom is."

Kate knocked Jasmine's hand away, suddenly furious. "It wasn't *me* who got Tom involved in all—"

"Save it, honey. Not interested." Jasmine's dark eyes blazed into Kate's. "However you dress it up, that boy was turned 'wolf because of you. You're trouble. Stuck-up, skinny-ass trouble."

Before Kate could open her mouth to utter another word, a nurse poked his tired head around the curtain. "You two—take any fights outside, please. You're disturbing the patients."

"We're done," said Jasmine. With a last glare at Kate she stalked away, pushing past the nurse. Kate listened to the click of her footsteps dwindle down the corridor.

Only when the noise had stopped and the nurse had gone back about his business did she allow the tears to fall.

Tom awoke from a familiar nightmare, sweating and itching inside. He'd been running in his lupine form, chasing after something that was always just out of view, never allowed to quit, his hunger building and building.

Groggily he sat up, his throat thick and filled with the iron tang of blood, like he'd had a nosebleed or something. It was his imagination, he knew, but the taste of it was maddening. On the table beside him was a little paper cup with a viscous red fluid inside. Stacy serum, he guessed. There was a note scrawled beside it: DRINK ME IF YOU NEED ME.

Tom drained the sticky mixture in one gulp, his head still spinning. It tasted like licorice but scalded his throat. "Half boy, half wolf, half guinea pig," he muttered.

"That's three halves," Kate said, pushing her head around the door.

"Once again I achieve the impossible." Tom looked up and did a double take. Kate's hair was now a vibrant red. "Hey, you look great!"

Kate wrinkled her nose. "You think? I'm not totally convinced." She pulled some strands around to scrutinize. "I guess I'll get used to it. . . ."

"Sure, you will." The burn in his throat was fading now, and he felt a lot brighter. "Anyway, aside from the hair, how's it going?"

"Don't ask," she said lightly.

Was it his imagination, or were Kate's eyes looking a little red too, like she'd been crying?

"As for *where* it's going," she added, "that's Baychester, Gun Hill Bridge. Get yourself ready."

Tom listened wide-eyed as Kate told him about Polar's call. "It could be a trap," he said. "Scratch that. It's *bound* to be a trap."

"I wanted to quiz Polar on the finer points," she said, "but Jasmine said no. Thinks I'm a bad influence on her friends."

Tom frowned. "What?"

"She's *such* a bitch," Kate said.

He didn't reply. But from the hurt way Kate looked at him, he realized he'd been supposed to. *Fell into that one,* he thought, and tried to fumble a reply, much too late.

Kate spoke over him. "*You* should try and call Polar," she suggested curtly. "Jasmine seems to like you a whole lot better."

"She does not," Tom protested.

"Oh, please. Just go ask her for the number."

"Well, where is she?"

"Losing your touch? Can't you go sniff her out or something?" Kate held up her hands even before he could register the hurt. "I'm sorry. Jesus, ignore me, okay? I'm just crabby, no sleep. . . ." She looked at him hopefully. "You understand . . . right? 'Cause Tom, if you don't understand me, I swear to God I don't know who ever could."

He looked at her for a few moments. Then he crossed the room and awkwardly reached out his arms to her. She rose and held him, and he clutched her back. Her body felt so good, so natural against his. . . .

A woman cleared her throat softly behind them. They sprang apart.

"Stacy," Tom said, a little flustered. "We were just—"

"Hey, no need to explain." Stacy smiled. "The new red hair's hot, right? I knew it was a good idea!"

Kate nodded awkwardly. "Yeah, I like it. Thanks, Stacy."

Stacy crossed to the table and checked the cup. "You took the serum, Tom. How're you feeling?"

"Fine." He blinked, considered for a moment. "Actually, I feel great. Better than I have for ages."

Stacy gave them a mischievous smile. "Sure that's not young love talking?"

"Ew." Kate shuddered, and they all laughed. "What's this about taking serum?"

"Later," Tom told her. "Stacy, do you know where Jasmine and Rico are?"

"They headed back home."

"Then we can't get ahold of Polar and check his story," Tom realized. "I don't have Jasmine's cell phone number."

Kate smiled sweetly. "What, you mean she hasn't given it to you already?"

They got directions from Stacy for riding the subway out to Baychester, as well as twenty dollars for expenses. "Pay me back in blood samples," she'd joked.

Kate had never seen Tom in such high spirits, cracking jokes, babbling about all kinds of nonsense, leapfrogging over trash cans. . . . She guessed he was excited at the thought of maybe meeting the man who could save his life—before the worst happened to his family. She waved her new hair in his face to remind him that as far as this whole city was concerned, they were wanted criminals; they should keep their profiles low.

"The cops'll never take me alive!" he shouted in a ridiculous gangster voice as he passed through the subway turnstile, drawing a gun from his fingers and pretending to shoot passersby.

"Okay, the infantile jerk thing is wearing a little thin now," Kate remarked. She was apprehensive, not just about what might be waiting for them in Baychester, but because of this change in Tom's behavior. What was happening with him? She'd been looking forward to spending a peaceful few hours together, just the two of them, before facing whatever lay ahead. But the new, hyper Tom apparently had no concept of quiet time. It had to be that serum stuff. He'd told her about taking it, and she'd scolded him for it: "There's no telling how it might affect someone like you."

"There *is* no one like me," he'd said darkly. "Remember?"

He calmed down a little once they got on the subway train. There were about a million stops. It was only five o'clock, but they'd figured if they got to the bridge early, they might get the jump on anyone trying to spring a nasty surprise. Plus, according to the map Stacy had loaned them, it might take that long to find a bus that would take them even close by.

Tom spent the rest of the journey catnapping, his newfound energy apparently spent. He woke up with a start every time the train lurched or screeched a little too loud, then sank back into a fitful slumber. *Good,* thought Kate. *Sleep it off.*

At last they arrived at their stop, deep in the Bronx. Neither of them said much while they waited for the bus to arrive, but it was a comfortable silence. As it turned out, they didn't have long to wait. The sun was low and dusky pink as a bus took them through a clean, urban landscape of malls and parks and schools; it certainly didn't look like the hotbed of crime and terror she'd heard about from movies and TV. But then, she had learned that few things were ever as they seemed.

Night had well and truly fallen by the time the bus dropped them off. With the time approaching seven-thirty, they crossed a cordoned-off stretch of parkland to reach Gun Hill Bridge. It was a dark, ornate structure that hunched long and low over the river below; the water resembled a strip of tarnished silver in the moonlight. An angular mass of scaffolding and tarps clung to one side of the bridge where it was in the process of being repaired. Streetlights stood flanking it like mute sentries, but they were broken and dark. Only one still shone, rooted in the middle of the bridge.

"Let's make for there," Tom said.

Kate agreed. "At least we'll be able to see who's coming."

As they crossed the dark bridge, Kate felt unease tease and itch at the back of her mind. It was too quiet out here. The solitary streetlight cast strange shadows as its light threaded the intricate ironwork of the balustrade below. Then Kate felt a shiver run through her. A dark figure was crouched at the foot of the streetlight.

It rose as they approached. The light glinted off a square of plastic in front of the figure's hooded face.

"Polar?" Kate shot a surprised glance at Tom. "What are you doing out here?"

"Where's Ramon?" Tom added. "Is he with you?"

Slowly Polar shook his head and lowered his camera. He pulled a Polaroid picture from the pocket of his gray sweatshirt and passed it to Kate in silence.

She angled it in the dim light to see what it was. Bile rose in her chest. Tom snatched the photo away for a closer look. Then he let it fall it to the ground.

"Oh my God," he said quietly.

It was a picture of Ramon, lying in a pool of blood, his throat slashed.

"Why?" Kate whispered shakily. "When did this . . . ?" She felt cut up inside. "Polar, for God's sake, what happened?"

She looked imploringly at the silent, hooded figure. And then she caught the yellow gleam in Polar's eyes.

"He's 'wolf, Tom," she murmured, backing away, panic rising. "They turned him. *He* did it."

"No, Kate. *I* did."

They spun around, though Kate knew who had spoken, knew who had crept up quietly behind them while they stood speechless in shock.

"Mom," she whispered.

CHAPTER TEN

"I guessed you would get here early," said Marcie Folan. Her smile was as cold and bleak as the moon above. "Sweetie, what has Mommy told you about dyeing your hair? Am I going to have to punish you?"

Kate said nothing. Tom stared at the scrawny woman facing them, her face pale, bloodless lips stretched tight over her teeth. The reek of death hung about her. Marcie Folan, the woman who had ripped his life apart, made him half animal, driven him into the darkness. She had wanted him dead since he'd first crossed her by accidentally killing Wesley, her 'wolf son, in a life-or-death struggle. But Takapa had stayed Tom's execution. He wanted Tom taken apart first. Cell by cell.

So what was Marcie's agenda now?

He thought of his parents, of Ramon, of all the people this woman had tainted or killed. It was all Tom could do not to throw himself at her, let the 'wolf inside him out to tear into her. But Kate must have seen the way he was tensing because she grabbed hold of his arm, held him back.

"No," she whispered. "Keep control. She wants to goad us into making mistakes."

Tom nodded slowly. Kate didn't sound very calm herself, but he knew she was right. "Where is my family?" he demanded.

Marcie's mocking laughter taunted him. "Why, here in New York, of course, while the manhunt for their murdering son continues."

"If you've hurt them—"

"They're safe for now," Marcie told him, voice smooth as honey. "How long they remain that way depends on your cooperation, naturally."

"Cooperation? With you?"

Her eyes gleamed faint yellow. "It's advisable, Tom. You've seen what happens to those who don't."

The photo he'd dropped was caught in a wintry gust and flapped about his feet. He clenched his fists. "Why Ramon? Why kill him?"

"I wanted him to call his friend, the girl, to summon you here. So much less suspicious than using that monosyllabic freak." She tutted. "But Ramon simply wouldn't make the call, whatever I did to him.

"I knew you'd suspect this was a trap," Marcie went on as two more dark figures advanced from out of the night behind her. "But then I realized it really didn't matter. With the carrot of Jicaque dangled in front of your faces, like donkeys you'd follow it anywhere."

"The carrot of Jicaque," echoed Tom, playing for time, trying to think through some way of escape. "That's some voodoo charm thing, right?"

Marcie smiled without humor. "Your friend Ramon acted brave too. Joking until the last. You should've heard the way he laughed when I opened his throat. . . ."

As she spoke, Tom glanced behind him. Polar was still hovering wraithlike beneath the streetlight. And from out of the shadows on the far side of the bridge two more people were advancing on them, hemming them in.

"And to think," Marcie continued with mock sadness, "that his skinny hide had just been patched up by that lush over on East 123rd. What a waste of sutures."

"So you know about Woollard," Tom said quietly.

"And his work," she added.

Kate frowned. "And you tolerate it?"

"Woollard and Stein both have their part to play in our plans," said Marcie. Her eyes gleamed. "Like you two. I'm so glad I've found you both again."

Tom was drawing a blank on any means of escape. He had to keep her talking, buy them some time. "How did you know we were even in contact with Ramon?"

Marcie assumed an innocent expression. "I didn't."

"I told her," said one of the dark figures, stepping forward into the better light. Tom had already recognized the voice and the massive frame, now wielding a baseball bat with a half-dozen nails knocked through the fat end. Swagger.

Kate took a sharp breath and Tom reached for her hand. She clutched him for a second, then let go. He watched her draw herself up to her full height and stare defiantly across at the towering man.

"You owe me, girl," Swagger said. "And I'm going to collect. Promise."

"I don't get it, Swagger," Tom said, trying to distract him. "You said you wanted Ramon alive."

Swagger answered, but his gaze still lingered greedily on Kate. "That was when he still had his gang and could lead them the way we wanted. Now they've scattered. We don't need him."

"And Polar was the consolation prize?"

"Turned him myself last night." Swagger grinned. "Thought I might need a spy."

"Good military thinking," said Marcie. "Now I understand why Takapa has made you his personal aide."

"Yeah, until now she couldn't believe that he'd hired such an ugly loser," Kate added helpfully.

"That's enough. Really, it's so cold out here. So exposed." Marcie fixed her eyes on Tom, then took a step toward him. Swagger and his heavy kept pace with her. "Takapa has private lodgings close by. Perhaps you'd care to accompany me there?"

"Nice offer," Tom said, "but we've made plans." He checked behind him and saw the other thugs were advancing closer too. Soon he and Kate would be trapped.

"Ah, *Tom*." Marcie pronounced his name with an odd relish. "If only you would give in to your lupine blood, overcome your resister's heritage. What a leader *you* would make."

"You wanted me dead before."

"My judgment was a little colored. . . . Takapa has studied the preliminary samples we took from you in New Orleans. There's a lot we can learn from you." Another step closer. "But do we really have to take your body's secrets from you by force? If you were to work with us, *help* us—we would spare your life and your family too."

"Don't listen to her," Kate snapped. "She's trying to trick you."

Tom's mind was racing. "And Kate?"

"She must do as she is told," said Marcie firmly. She took another step closer. "We *must* continue our bloodline, Tom."

"She'll give me to Takapa." Kate's voice was high and forced. "She'll have me raped."

"I prefer the phrase 'force mated,'" said Marcie, eyes shining. "To cement the union of our ideals, the forging of our beautiful lupine future."

Unable to go forward or back, Tom and Kate edged toward the side of the bridge, where the top of the scaffolding peeped over the rail, their one teasing hope of escape.

Marcie, Swagger, and the others began to close in on them. Only Polar hung back, still clutching his camera.

"She's won, Kate," Tom said bitterly.

Kate stared at him in disbelief. "Tom, no!"

Suddenly for a split second the bridge was lit up with a blinding flash—Polar, to Tom's left, had taken another picture.

"You freak!" Swagger shouted, rubbing his eyes.

In that moment Tom and Kate acted.

Kate kicked her mother in the stomach. Marcie screeched and fell back.

At the same time Tom wrested the bat from Swagger's hands. It was a gruesome weapon. But what choice did he have? He hefted its weight, hands sweaty, arms tingling. A strange tinge of red blurred across his vision. He swung the bat at Swagger.

Swagger took a hard blow to the head. He shouted out and crumpled to the ground. One of the heavies grabbed Tom around the neck, but Tom shoved the spiked end of the bat up into his attacker's face. The thug cried out in pain, staggered, and fell. Tom kicked him to make sure he stayed down. Kate screamed, but he ignored her, swung the bat again and knocked another thug's legs from under him, felt the nails snag on clothing and flesh, wrenched them free with vicious satisfaction.

"Tom!" Kate was screaming. It sounded like she was a hundred miles away.

The fourth of Swagger's thugs was running away back down the bridge, Polar close behind him, ignoring Marcie's demands that they stand their ground.

Marcie. She must be sprawling somewhere in the reddening shadows. Tom peered about for her, clutching the bat tight in his sweating hands. Now he could make her pay; now he would—

"Drop it!" Kate had grabbed him by the shoulders, was shrieking in his face. She was covered in blood. "Tom, for God's sake, *please* drop it!"

Suddenly the weapon felt white-hot in his hands. He let it clatter to the ground. "Are you . . . ?" He felt dizzy, sick to his stomach. Her cheek and neck were sticky and dark. "Are you okay, Kate? You're bleeding. . . ."

"It's not *my* blood, Tom," she wailed, "it's *theirs*." She pointed to Swagger, clutching his head and gasping, and the two thugs who were writhing on the ground in agony.

"I . . . I wanted to kill them." Tom stared at them. "I mean, *really* wanted to."

"You were never like this before." Kate hugged herself. "It's that stuff Stacy gave you; it must be!"

"Jesus . . ." Tom started to shake. Tears welled up and streaked down his cheeks. "I couldn't stop myself. . . ."

"Enough," snarled Marcie. Her eyes were yellow and bright, her features beginning to buckle and shift.

Swagger was pushing himself up onto his hands and knees. His eyes were shut, his forehead gashed open. Tom watched as thick, coarse hair started to sprout from the wound.

"This way!" Kate shouted as she jumped up onto the wide metal rail that ran along the side of the bridge. "Tom, come on. Come *on*. The 'wolves can't climb."

Kate swung herself down onto the top bar of the steel scaffolding against the bridge's side and began to climb down to the planks below.

A low, rumbling noise behind him drew Tom's dazed attention. He looked back over his shoulder.

The dark, nightmarish shape of Marcie in 'wolf form came howling out of the darkness toward him, her foaming jaws wide open and ready to devour. Swagger ran beside her, a hulking, hideous creature, his sandy coat matted and bloody.

Tom leapt onto the scaffolding after Kate.

But as he swung down to the next level, he landed badly and started to fall. He grabbed hold of a corner of the thick tarp that shrouded the metal scaffold. It ripped under his weight but slowed his descent—before one of the scaffolding bars stopped it completely as he landed astride it. Pain tore through his body. He struggled to rise, to haul himself up onto one of the planks, but he was tangled in the tarp.

A hot, itching feeling began to surge through his body; his head started to pound. The urge to change. But there was something different. The compulsion, usually nagging and insistent, was all-engulfing. *They want you to give in to your wolf side? Okay. Fine. Show them just what that means.* That weird red tint was back in his vision. "Kate," he gasped. "Help me."

"Hold on, Tom," she called, from somewhere close by.

A terrifying, keening howl echoed out around him.

"No, Tom!" Kate called desperately. "Please, no, not now! Not like this!"

It suddenly clicked in his head that the howling was his. The change was in full flow. His human flesh and bones were melting away as his 'wolf lunged out from the darkness to dominate. Tom could feel his consciousness slipping away as the lupine will took hold.

"Your eyes," Kate was shouting, almost hysterical. "Jesus, Tom, your eyes are yellow! *Yellow! This isn't you, Tom, it isn't you!*"

CHAPTER ELEVEN

Tom's morphing lupine body tore free of Ramon's clothes. His body looked more bestial, more powerful than Kate had ever seen it.

This wasn't Tom as she knew him. She could *hear* it in the way he bellowed his rage up at Marcie and Swagger. The two 'wolves were leaning over the side of the bridge above them, jaws snapping, their sinister silhouettes blotting out the cloudy sky.

Kate had seen the rage that had taken Tom up on the bridge, the violence he'd meted out. The glazed, unseeing look in his eyes. Now that rage was back—only in his 'wolf form, Tom could be unstoppable.

He leapt down from the scaffolding and landed half on land, half in the water. At once two black shapes detached themselves from the darkness and attacked him. Jesus, there were more 'wolves down there, lying in wait—they'd been surrounded. Clearly her mother was taking no chances.

But just as clearly Marcie hadn't reckoned with the change in Tom's personality. Kate saw her standing motionless now, watching the show as Tom fought off the 'wolves with a ruthless determination. His club-like paws swiped through flesh. His teeth tore at fur and muscle and bone.

It was a bloodbath.

Another 'wolf burst out of the blackness to throw itself at Tom, and he went down beneath its bulk. The two monsters rolled till they hit the water with a colossal splash. Kate stared helplessly.

While Marcie was distracted, Kate moved down through the planks and poles of the scaffolding as quietly as she could, then jumped into a clump of long, springy grass. Yet another 'wolf raced by to join the fray but too quickly to register her presence. She hated the thought of running out on Tom—but what could she possibly do for him now?

She considered running cross-country in the direction they'd come, but it was wide-open parkland—if she were spotted, they'd bring her down in moments. There was woodland the other way. At least it would give her cover while she waited for Tom to calm down and come find her.

With a shudder she crept beneath the bridge. It was almost pitch black, but if she could just pick her way through to the other side . . .

A low growling ahead of her told her she'd made a terrible mistake.

Out from the shadows came a massive 'wolf. But the shape of it, the smell of it . . .

Her heart lurched. "Daddy."

His glowing eyes bored into her; his salivating jaws opened.

Hot tears prickled Kate's eyes. "Please, Daddy," she pleaded. "Please let me go."

The 'wolf that was her father stared at her for what felt like forever.

Then he turned and slunk away.

Kate stood like a statue in the darkness. Maybe some things were stronger than 'wolf bloodlust. "Thank you," she whispered.

She heard the lupine baying and snarling up ahead of her grow fainter. Her father was leading the other 'wolves away.

Suddenly she could hear something else: the droning note of a car engine and the rattling of a chassis as it bumped and scraped over uneven ground. Kate's heart leapt. But whipped up into such a frenzy, would the 'wolves retreat—or simply attack anyone who dared come near?

She got her answer a few seconds later in the form of a ululating animal wail close by. It was her mother, crying out in impotent rage. The strange acoustics beneath the bridge took the sound and twisted it, made it echo and re-echo unbearably— but while it half deafened Kate, the effect it had on the 'wolves was more profound. She saw their shadowy forms shift fleetly past the bridge, answering the keening call, heard heavy footfalls and scuffling all around. They were being summoned away, back into the cold shadows that harbored them.

Kate waited a few seconds more, then emerged from her hiding place. The dark landscape seemed suspiciously still, the only sound the engine of the slowly approaching vehicle. Then she gasped as something broke the surface of the shallow water.

It was Tom, naked and shivering cold, staring around in confusion.

He saw her, covered himself with both hands, and stumbled toward her. "I'm sorry," he murmured, his voice slurred like he'd been drinking. "Kate, I'm so sorry." He collapsed to his knees on the chill wet grass. "Kate, what's happening to me?"

He looked at her so helplessly that she ran to him and held him tight. His skin was corpse cold, ridged with deep cuts and scrapes from his struggle. His shivering got more violent; Kate guessed he was in shock. "You're back," she whispered soothingly in his ear. "It's over now."

He hugged her closer. "Is it?" he murmured.

The car had stopped, and she heard its door slam shut. "Tom? Kate?"

She could have cheered, or cried, or collapsed with relief. Stacy Stein had come looking for them. "Down here!" Kate called. "And do you have a blanket in your car?"

Stacy appeared over the rise of the bridge with a flashlight.

"Oh my God!" Stacy cried. "Are you guys okay?"

Tom looked up into the beam of light. Kate saw him force the tiniest of smiles through his chattering teeth.

"Take me to your heater," he said.

The warm air pumped out on full as Stacy drove them away from Gun Hill Bridge in her battered Ford, back to civilization. Tom was curled up on the backseat, sleeping now beneath a plaid blanket.

Kate sat beside Stacy in the front, checking the mirror every few seconds to be sure no one was following. "Thank you, Stacy," she murmured for the twentieth time. "If you hadn't come when you did . . ."

Stacy waved away her gratitude. "Would they have killed you?"

Kate closed her eyes. "I don't know what they would've done." She outlined what had happened on the bridge—including Tom's reaction to the serum.

"I can't understand why it should have affected him that way," Stacy muttered. "The serum contains agents that excite certain parts of the brain—it gives a lupine all the rush of the hunt and the kill without the need to make it happen for real."

"Well, this was for real," Kate said with a shudder.

"After delivering the rush a downer kicks in, a pacifier," Stacy continued. She cursed softly. "Why should it have such an effect on Tom? Something to do with his wereling chemistry?"

"I saw Swagger and his generals take some of

143

that serum," Kate said. "It didn't pacify *them* either. If anything, it made them more hostile."

"Maybe I need to perform further tests."

Kate heard the weariness in Stacy's voice, the reluctance to believe she could've gotten things so wrong—and to face the ramifications of that mistake. "Maybe," she agreed. "Stacy, how did you know the message we got was a fake?"

"I got a call from Jicaque after you left. He wanted to meet up with Tom."

"What?" Suddenly Tom was wide awake.

"And *only* Tom. Midnight, some place off Times Square." Stacy shrugged. "I knew one of the messages had to be bogus. The only way to find out was to come out here and get you."

"How do we know we can trust this *other* Jicaque?" Kate said bitterly.

"He said something kind of weird about Tom. . . ." Stacy clicked her tongue as she tried to remember. "Oh yeah—'This time put on your pants *before* we meet.'" She frowned. "Make any sense?"

"It's him," Tom said, struggling forward under his blanket so he could better talk to Stacy. "We first met in New Orleans. . . . I'd changed back from the 'wolf and I ducked into some scuzzy old movie theater to get dressed. He was sitting there—turned out he owned the place—and asked me if I needed any help. I didn't know it was him till way after. . . . No one else would know that happened."

Kate nodded. "And if my mother had gotten to him, why would she arrange a message to be left while she was tricking us out to Gun Hill?" She looked at him. "Jesus, Tom. *He's* found *us*."

"Or Tom, anyway," said Stacy. "The message was for Tom to meet him at some diner called Vegetarian Kitchen."

"I guess that's a good sign," Tom said. "Sorry you can't come."

"Maybe he's scared of my mom—wants nothing to do with her daughter . . ." Kate said, trailing off as a horrible thought struck her. "Oh God, I just realized. Someone's got to tell Rico and Jasmine . . . about Ramon."

"Rico's brother?" Stacy asked sharply. "What about him?"

Kate opened her mouth to tell her, but the words wouldn't come. It didn't seem possible that someone as larger-than-life as Ramon could now be gone. She turned to Tom, her eyes misting over. All she could see was the Polaroid image of Ramon's desecrated body.

"It's bad news," Tom said huskily.

The mood in the car was subdued as they drove into the seething heart of New York. Tom was guiltily glad to have gotten away and grateful that it was Kate who would be breaking the news about Ramon.

He felt oddly detached from his surroundings as

he wandered down Broadway. Everywhere was bright and well lit. People surged along the wide-open streets in great waves, spewing out from theaters and restaurants in hundreds. Great skyscrapers shot up from out of the busy traffic on every street in sight. And as he finally came to Times Square, there was a sense of something truly giant in the air—not just the neon billboards cranked up high over the city, or the TV screens the size of condos, or the buildings that outstretched and outshone the night sky. There was a brash, rough-and-ready optimism about the place, the feeling that *anything* was possible.

Tom tried to give himself up to the feeling, but he was still coming to terms with the wild mood swings he'd felt since taking the serum. He kept getting flashbacks, frozen moments of violence that stung his senses. He hoped that he'd ridden out the side effects and was normal again—at least, as normal as possible.

He'd hated the lupine nature within him before, but if he could no longer control the beast and its power . . .

At least he felt warmer now. Luckily Stacy had remembered a tip from one of the street kids in her program: a thrift store on Broadway dumped unwelcome donations outside with its trash. Kate had managed to find him a holey sweater, a threadbare tweed jacket, and a pair of tuxedo pants sporting some very suspect stains. They went nicely with the grubby pair of basketball shoes, straight out of the eighties and a size too small.

His fashion sense was the least of his worries, whatever the smirking hordes thronging the sidewalks around him might think. His stomach was fizzing with nerves at the thought of meeting Jicaque after so many tricks, so many false hopes. . . .

It was five minutes to midnight. Tom found his steps quickening as he turned onto West 44th Street. Did he dare to think he really could be cured?

The Vegetarian Kitchen was a tiny bistro between a 7-Eleven and a tacky video store.

It was closed.

Tom stared at it in disbelief. There was no doubt about it: the place was dark, empty, shut up for the night.

"Hey," a man's voice whispered close by. "Down here."

The voice was coming from an alleyway that ran beside the bistro. His hopes igniting once more, Tom rushed to the mouth of the dark alley to investigate.

Someone grabbed hold of his jacket and dragged him inside. He cried out, but a hand clamped over his mouth. *The 'wolves,* he thought, panicking. *How could I have been so stupid?*

Across from the alleyway on the other side of the street a psychic advertised her services in gaudy, flickering neon. In its pink burn he saw a man, Asian, lurking in the thick shadows.

Tom bit the thick fingers bruising his lips, and with a grunt the man snatched them away. But before Tom could shout for help, the Asian doubled him up with a punch in the stomach and thrust a knife toward his face.

The other man grabbed Tom again, this time in a neck lock.

"Give us your money and don't make a sound or we'll make you bleed, kid."

"Muggers?" Tom gasped. Bizarrely he felt a rush of sudden relief. "Thank God."

He saw the Asian frown. "Huh?"

Tom tried to catch his breath. Okay, so they might not be 'wolves—but the city had dangers enough without them, and he had been a fool to forget it. "I don't have any money . . ." he spluttered. "All I have is the clothes I'm in. Look at me. . . ."

Change, he thought. *Change to save yourself. . . .*

The knife man frisked him quickly. "Nothing." Then he smiled and held the knife to Tom's cheek. "Maybe we'll take something else from you, huh?"

Change!

Tom thought of the hundreds of people on those bright-lit streets just steps away. After what happened at Gun Hill, he knew he couldn't risk their lives to save his own.

And since his last hope had finally failed him, why fight? Maybe it was time just to give in at last.

He shut his eyes as the knifepoint pressed into his cheek.

Then a clang echoed around the alleyway, and the knife fell away. A hand reached past Tom's face and jabbed at the man who held him. With a cry of pain the man fell back, clutching his eyes.

The muggers ran down the alleyway and back to the main drag.

Tom stared in disbelief at his rescuer. An aging Native American whose silver hair hung down to his shoulders in scruffy braids. His face was lined, his nose like a big, straight arrow through the contours, pointing down to a cleft chin. His eyes were amber in the light, twinkling with amusement.

The old man held up a glistening hand. "Chili oil," he announced in a voice that held no trace of accent. He gestured to a door in the wall beside him. "From the kitchens. I think it stung his eyes a little."

Tom noticed the heavy frying pan in the man's other hand. "You hit the guy with that?" he asked.

"The use of force is unfortunate," his rescuer commented, "but sometimes necessary." He paused. "Greetings, Tom Anderson."

"Jicaque?" asked Tom, shell shocked.

"Sometimes," agreed the old man almost regretfully. "I prefer being Johnny Oldman, lately arrived in Manhattan as deputy head chef of the Vegetarian Kitchen." He brightened. "My egg rolls are the finest in Midtown."

Tom just stared at him dumbly.

"But what am I thinking?" the old man went on. "You need a strong cup of java. I know someplace we can go."

The old man headed back to the street, still clutching the frying pan.

Tom watched him go, his spirit shaken. This daffy old guy was really Jicaque, fabled medicine man and scourge of 'wolves across the country?

Heavyhearted, Tom was about to follow him when he noticed the door in the wall leading to the kitchen of the restaurant. It was bolted shut and secured with a large padlock. So how the hell had Jicaque gotten out here?

With a shiver of anticipation Tom followed the old man as he turned left toward the hustle of the brighter streets.

Kate dreaded the task ahead of her as Stacy turned the car into the street where Ramon had his hideout. She'd tried rehearsing what she was going to tell Jasmine and Rico, but the words kept coming out all wrong.

Something else was wrong too.

A sleek, dark stretch limousine was parked outside the slum tenements. It looked incongruous with the housing projects crowding the skyline behind it.

"That's weird," Stacy observed, slowing down. "What would a limo be doing here?"

"Look," Kate said. "There's someone coming down the steps." A stooped, bedraggled-looking man was trudging down the steps leading to the hangout. Something glinted in his hand; metal or glass perhaps, but she couldn't tell what.

"That's Dr. Woollard," Stacy reported. "I didn't think he ever left his house; why would he come to Ramon's now?"

She was about to honk the horn to attract his attention, but Kate grabbed her by the wrist to stop her. "Oh my God," she whispered. "Look."

A figure had emerged from the limousine to greet Woollard. He was ghoulish looking, deathly pale, his features bunched up in the middle of his pockmarked face. His white-blond hair was shaved back to stubble. As he ushered Woollard into the back of the car, he smiled, baring a sharp set of teeth.

"Takapa," Kate breathed. "The one who's making all this happen."

Stacy nodded. "Looks like Woollard's joined up with him."

"God help us," Kate whispered.

CHAPTER TWELVE

Tom glanced around the coffee shop while Jicaque placed their order at the counter. Scattered tables of twenty-somethings huddled together over the yellow Formica. Middle-aged men stared out stoically through the menu-cluttered windows, seemingly reluctant to go home to their empty apartments. A lovelorn couple, he too young and she too old, gazed at each other over untouched lattes. Tom felt oddly at home here, just one more person in the coffee shop crowd hiding from the sharp truths of life for a few short hours.

Jicaque returned, placing a cup of coffee in front of Tom. "You're disappointed," he noted, sitting opposite Tom in the grimy booth. "You were expecting someone more impressive, right?"

"No," Tom protested.

His companion smiled wryly. "And a bad liar. But you, more than most, should appreciate that outward appearances count for little. At least in the world that *we* inhabit." He took a packet of cigarettes from his pocket. "Take these."

"No thanks, I don't smoke."

"I mean take them by way of example. I am an old man now, and I have survived the attentions of many enemies only through being prepared." Jicaque's smile grew wilier, and he lowered his voice. "I don't always carry a frying pan, and I don't smoke, either. But I carry cigarettes powdered with a special compound of magnesium. Should I find myself in trouble, I take out a cigarette and light it. The resultant flare is a useful distraction."

"Ouch," Tom said. "Should I be worried about this coffee?"

"At fifty cents a cup, maybe we both should," Jicaque replied.

Some oldster music, jazz or something, was piping through little speakers in the corners of the room. Jicaque clearly approved, shaking his head in time to the shifting beat. "Stan Getz," he said with a sigh of contentment. "Pure genius. You know his work?"

"I think maybe my dad's heard of him," Tom said.

"Kids." The old man grimaced, then sipped his coffee. "Won't you drink?"

Tom felt dazed. He had thought of this momentous meeting so many times; somehow he'd never imagined it would take place over a Formica table with corny old records playing in the background. He shrugged, raised the cup to his lips, and sipped.

Jicaque watched him intently, expectantly.

"It's good, thanks," Tom said, remembering his

manners. Jicaque went on staring, and Tom shifted uncomfortably. "Do I have a coffee mustache or something?"

"Hmmm," the old man said at last. "The powder I just slipped in your drink would have made you violently ill by now if you weren't what I believe you to be."

Tom stared at his coffee cup in alarm, then half rose to his feet. "There's poison in this?"

"No," said Jicaque mildly, glancing around to check that no one had overheard. "Just a combination of dried herbs—an old, old recipe." His expression hardened. "I heard many rumors about you. I'm careful what I choose to believe. If not, I would've been killed years ago."

Tom sat back down warily and pushed aside his coffee. "Maybe I should be more careful too. I heard you'd retired from practicing medicine."

Jicaque smiled, his amber-colored eyes twinkling. "So the 'wolves like to think. You could say I started minding their business a little too closely. The lupine community does not appreciate human interference in its affairs. They threatened to kill me."

"They're evil," Tom said. "They should be wiped out. Hunted down."

Jicaque shook his head. "Like any predator, they have the right to exist." He sighed. "Were-wolves have been a part of the fabric of human society for countless generations. But they weren't always hidden. Want to hear an old man's story?"

Tom nodded. "It has to beat the jazz."

Jicaque frowned at him, then began his tale. "No one knows for sure when the first werewolf dragged itself out of the darkness and into the world of men. According to the ancient texts, a community of Pueblo people in America's Southwest suffered particularly from a plague of attacks. As is often the case in nature, they discovered a natural remedy. If the bitten victim took a solution of a local herb—in any other situation highly toxic—for one lunar month, then the lupine toxins were unable to take hold. Ancient magic and rites were used to support a body's natural resistance as it used the herb to overcome the lupine threat."

Tom's eyebrows drew together. "So it's sort of like the herb helped the bitten person create antibodies."

Jicaque nodded. "Eventually babies began to be born with natural immunity. After that, the community was able to drive out the lupine entirely."

He paused to take another sip from his cup. "They came to be known as the Shipapi, taking their name from the Pueblo word *Shipap,* meaning the womb of the earth, the place from which the first pure human beings entered the world."

"Go on," Tom said, fascinated.

"Slowly the word spread to other tribes that there was a way to fight back against wolfkind. But because the 'wolves hid in human form, the Shipapi's secrets were entrusted only to a very few. They traveled the land, driving out the hidden 'wolves and appointing others in this sacred order."

"So what went wrong?" Tom reached to take another gulp of his coffee—then changed his mind. "How'd the 'wolf fight back?"

Jicaque smiled grimly. "It's the old story—human arrogance. The Shipapi grew complacent; their natural protection was diluted through careless mating. The 'wolves were finally able to infiltrate the ranks of the Shipapi. Trust dwindled, and so too did the numbers of the Shipapi. So many people died. . . ." Abruptly Jicaque stopped, staring into space. A tear welled, glistened in his eye.

"Are you okay?" Tom whispered.

"Sorry. It's just this sax break here. . . ." He tapped his skinny chest. "Gets me every time, you know?"

Tom rolled his eyes. "Look . . . you're telling a great story, but what does it have to do with what's happening now?"

"Be patient," said Jicaque sharply. "Though the natural immunity of the Shipapi was seriously compromised, resistance, in various forms and levels, still occurred in subsequent generations. It's still evident today in a few individuals." Now the old man smiled. "The 'wolves call these *silverbloods*. You've heard of the expression?"

Tom felt the hairs on the back of his neck prickle. *He* had been called a silverblood. "I'm descended from the Shipapi?" he asked in wonder. "You mean, like, my great-great-great-great-grandfather was one of those people?"

Jicaque hesitated as a departing couple passed by close to their table.

"Yes, you carry the blood of the ancient guardians," Jicaque said softly. "A little diluted, sure—but there nonetheless."

Tom grimaced. "Not strong enough," he said. "Marcie Folan still made a newblood out of me."

"Not entirely; she made you a *wereling,*" Jicaque pointed out. "As for me, I carry the resistance in a purer form."

"Like Rico," Tom guessed. Jicaque looked blank. "This kid I know," Tom went on. "His blood is poison to the 'wolves; he can't be turned."

"Like Rico, indeed," Jicaque observed. "But unlike Rico and unlike you, I have been aware of my Shipapi inheritance all my life. I was sworn to watch the 'wolves, to help limit their numbers for the sake of humanity—and their own survival."

"So how have you gone about it?" Tom asked him.

"Traveled from place to place, guided by others of the ancient order," Jicaque replied. "If a lupine community was turning too many newbloods, I would try to cure some of them, restore the proper balance."

157

Tom finally spoke aloud the question he'd been steeling himself to ask: "So you *can* cure people who've been turned 'wolf?"

"If a lupine wishes to embrace his humanity once more, then yes," Jicaque agreed.

"Can you cure me?"

"I can," he said simply.

Tom sat back, stunned. "Wow." Was this it? Could it really be so simple?

Jicaque sighed deeply. "I'm scared," he added. "I don't want the 'wolves to kill me. For a while I even turned my back on my calling and went into hiding." This time the tears brimming in his tired old eyes were for real. "You're right to be disappointed in me. By turning a blind eye I've allowed Takapa's evil to fester and grow. The lupine community has traditionally survived by restricting its activities, hunting only when need is at its greatest, scattering its members throughout the population."

"But Takapa wants to swell the numbers," Tom said.

"Yes," the old man said. "He seeks to lead his kind out from the darkness. His activities in this city are in preparation for that day. And it's not far from now." Jicaque looked at Tom, his face inscrutable. "I *can* cure you, Tom. But if I'm going to fight Takapa, I need powerful allies."

Tom felt uneasy. He sensed what was coming.

"You have great powers," Jicaque went on.

"Surrender them now and I fear for your safety and that of Kate and your family."

"But Takapa wants me for research. If I was just human again, it would wreck his plans, wouldn't it?"

"Perhaps," Jicaque agreed. "But Marcie Folan will still want revenge, Tom. She will come for you. And have you forgotten you're still wanted for murder?"

"You think showing the court I'm a werewolf will count in my defense?" Tom shook his head wearily. "You're the wise old medicine man; help me out here. Kate's in danger. My whole family's in danger. How can I keep them safe?"

"If Takapa's plans succeed, who will be safe?" Jicaque placed his gnarled old hands over Tom's own. "I sense the strength in you." A flicker passed over his tanned, lined face. "And I sense the balance in you has shifted recently. You must hold on to the good, Tom. Hold on to the good."

Tom felt a chill pass down his spine. "I . . . I took some kind of drug," he said. "It was supposed to suppress the lupine in me, to control the bloodlust, but instead . . ." He shuddered. "*I* lost control. Stacy Stein and Dr. Woollard, they must've got the research wrong. They—"

Jicaque pulled his hands away. "Woollard, you say?"

Tom nodded. "He's a doctor over in Harlem, a blood specialist; sometimes helps Stacy out. Do you know him?"

"No. But I've come across the name before," Jicaque replied. "Originated in Saxon England. It means 'guardian of wolves.' A name given by the Shipapi to humans sympathetic to the ways of the 'wolf."

"Coincidence," Tom said uneasily. "It must be. Stacy's working to develop a *cure* for the lupine toxin." He glared at Jicaque. "And *you've* had the knowledge all along. You could've helped her for real, not just sent over a bunch of herbs."

"It's not up to me whether a race should die or live," Jicaque retorted. "I just try to preserve the proper balances. Dr. Stein wants to *control* life through her . . . *chemicals*." He spoke the word with a grimace, like it was somehow disgusting.

"She's trying to help newbloods control their cravings," Tom said fiercely. "While you were burying your head in the sand, Takapa turned a whole lot of kids 'wolf. Too many. It's a bloodbath waiting to happen, and that's what Stacy's trying to prevent."

"I know it," said Jicaque quietly. "But *suppose* . . . suppose her good work has been perverted in some way?"

"But who could have . . . ?" Tom trailed off, his breath catching in his throat. "Woollard?"

Jicaque met his worried gaze evenly. "Think of the effect this concoction had on *you*."

"Then I've got to warn Stacy," Tom realized, jumping to his feet. "Right now."

"Yes," Jicaque agreed, rising as well and nodding

farewell to the man behind the counter. "And I'd better prepare."

"Prepare?" Tom frowned, following him out of the coffee shop and onto the neon-soaked sidewalk outside. A light rain was falling, and people hurried by with their heads down, their coats clutched close. "What do you mean, prepare?"

"The bloodbath you mentioned," Jicaque replied grimly, "has to be stopped. Whatever the cost."

Tom peered out into the road. "Do you have money for a cab?" he asked Jicaque, trying to spy any yellow in the traffic. "I've got to get to Ramon's hangout, quick—"

But when he turned back, he found that the medicine man had vanished.

"Jicaque?" He spun around, scanning the sidewalk, picking through the frantic figures fleeing the rain, but there was no sign of him. How could the old guy have moved so fast?

Then Tom realized someone was watching him, too. A cop, staring at him hard through the downpour, like he was trying to remember something.

"Hey!" the cop shouted. "Hey, you, hold it!"

Tom turned and splashed off down the street, muttering under his breath: "Teenage kid wanted on a charge of murder one and crimes against fashion. . . ."

Kate walked gingerly into the hangout to find Jasmine and Rico sitting together in front of the dark screen of the smashed TV. Stacy was close behind her, taking in the squalid conditions without apparent shock. Kate guessed she'd seen worse places than this in her time in the city.

"Are you guys okay?" Stacy asked.

"Jeez," said Jasmine, jumping in surprise. "Rico, man, you are popular tonight."

"Hey!" Rico looked delighted to see them. "Kate, you got red hair!"

She shrugged, self-conscious.

"You still cute, though." The boy grinned. "Guess what? I know where Tom's mom and dad are staying." He gestured excitedly through the archway that led to the next room, where Kate could hear the police radio squawk and splutter. "Cops was talking about some other conference or something tomorrow, picking them up next morning from a hotel on Madison. Room 3003."

"That's great news, Rico, well done!" Kate saw a tiny Band-Aid on Rico's arm just above the elbow. "Hey, what did Woollard want here?"

"What all doctors want," Rico complained. "Blood, blood, blood."

Stacy smiled in sympathy. "But why'd he come here, sweetheart?"

"Don't you know?" Jasmine frowned. "Lady, they're *your* samples." When Stacy looked blank, she went on, speaking slowly like the woman was stupid: "He took those samples for *you*."

162

"No, he didn't." Stacy looked worriedly at Kate. "Why would he come around here tonight?"

"Maybe because Tom got away?" Kate's mind was racing. "Mom said Takapa wanted Tom for testing, but maybe he's decided Rico's DNA will do in the meantime?"

Stacy nodded. "Whatever, Woollard's got some explaining to do. Maybe I should go see him."

"Takapa's dangerous," Kate warned. "If he's there—"

"Hey! Would you mind telling us just what the hell you're talking about?" Jasmine said irritably. "In any case, where's Ramon and Polar? And Tom?"

Kate felt her stomach ball itself up.

Rico turned his big eyes on her. "Doc Woollard said they'd gone to meet you."

She looked helplessly at Stacy. "Uh . . . Well . . ."

Jasmine looked at her uneasily. "You got something to say, say it."

Kate took a deep breath. "Tom went to meet someone. The *real* Jicaque."

"What do you mean, the *real* Jicaque?"

"That message Polar gave you . . . was a fake. He sold us out. He's one of them now. Swagger turned him last night." The words ground out of her mouth mechanically. "And . . . Ramon's dead. He was . . . The 'wolves killed him."

"Dead?" Rico's eyes filled with tears. "No way." He turned to Jasmine. "He's not dead, right? Right?"

Jasmine's eyes had zeroed in on Kate's. "How'd Ramon die?" When Kate didn't respond, she asked again, louder, angrier: *"How'd he die?"*

"Swagger told . . ." Kate drew a shuddering breath. "He told my mom she could get to me and Tom through Ramon. But Ramon wouldn't betray us. So . . . so . . ."

"I knew it," Jasmine hissed. Her eyes glittered. "You got him killed. *You.*"

"That's not fair, Jasmine," Stacy said gently.

"Oh, right," the girl sneered, her face contorted with rage. "You white girls, you got to stick together, right?"

"That's crap and you know it," Stacy snapped.

"No crap." Jasmine rose to her feet and crossed the room, then grabbed Kate by the arms and shook her. "*You* killed him!" she shouted. "Hear me? *Hear me?*"

Kate didn't react, just stood there and took it, so numb she could barely feel the girl's fingers digging into her flesh.

"Jasmine, stop it." Stacy tried to come between them. "This isn't helping; you have to—" But Jasmine knocked her away.

"You killed him!" Jasmine shrieked again in Kate's face. "If he'd never met you, he'd be here right now."

"Let her alone, Jas!" Rico's voice was high and clear. "If Ramon never met Kate and Tom, he'd be dead in Central Park. Or maybe dead from Swagger last night. Or maybe alive, sure—who knows? But he's dead now." The kid looked up at Kate, wiping his nose, and his voice grew small and quiet. "He's dead for real . . . right?"

Kate met Jasmine's glare. "Right," she breathed. "And I'm so, so sorry."

"Quiet, all of you," Stacy snapped. "Listen." The gravity in her voice made even Jasmine relinquish her grip and listen.

A nasal voice was crackling out from the police radio: ". . . fits the description of youth wanted in connection with the New Orleans homicide inquiry. Units in vicinity of West 44th and 10th, apprehend Caucasian male, black pants, tweed jacket. Proceed with caution. . . ."

"Oh my God, they're after Tom," Kate said. "If the police get ahold of him . . ." She didn't dare finish the sentence.

"What can we do?" said Stacy.

"Easy," Jasmine said shakily, wiping her eyes. "I'll go get him in the wagon."

Kate looked at her uncertainly. "You're in no state to drive anywhere."

"You here in my skin with me? You want to argue about this so long that the cops get Tom and he winds up dead like Ramon?"

"Then let me come with you," Kate insisted.

"No way," Jasmine said fiercely, shoving Kate

aside. "Come on, Rico." She grabbed the boy by the hand and dragged him out with her.

Kate went to follow, but Stacy stopped her. "Let her go. Let her cool off and work through some stuff."

"But she won't be thinking straight," Kate protested. "She could—"

"She doesn't need to think right now," Stacy replied. "Let's face it—she's got more experience with this kind of thing than we do."

"So what are *we* supposed to do?" Kate gestured to the radio. "Hang out and listen to the running commentary?"

"We go to Woollard's," said Stacy firmly. "Waiting around here won't do us any good, and it won't help Tom either."

"But if there's any news—"

"Jasmine will come find us, with Tom in tow, I'm sure," Stacy told her. "We'll leave a note." She pulled a small notepad and pen from her purse and gave them to Kate, who left a hasty scribble on the paper. "Now, come on. I've gone forty-eight hours without sleep. I could use some answers, you know?"

"I know," Kate said as she followed Stacy out. "So could I."

Tom's lungs burned. His sides were splitting and his legs felt leaden, but he kept on going, kept pushing his body harder. If he stopped now, he would never have the strength to set off again.

He'd scaled some tall gates and cut across a school playground, hoping he'd find somewhere to hide—but there seemed to be a cop car waiting around every street corner. Whichever alleyway he ducked down, there was a man in blue racing up it toward him. His ears were ringing with the shriek of sirens.

The city itself seemed to be caging him in: the skyscrapers, stone and glass and metal monoliths, were ranged up around him on every side. The rain poured down through a jigsaw piece of night, the only sky visible beyond the buildings' reach. Tom was soaked through, his feet cramped and blistered from his ill-fitting thrift store sneakers, but still he kept on running, *running*.

He vaulted a low fence and, with the last of his strength, sprinted into a parking lot. His footfalls on the wet concrete were so loud, he couldn't hear a single other thing. So at last he let himself stop, nauseous with exertion, wheezing for breath. His legs cramped up and he collapsed to his knees, breathing out steam in the freezing rain.

Willing himself to recover, he took a cautious look around him. The lot was quiet and still. If he could just get inside one of those cars, maybe he could hide out till morning and—

"Police! Freeze!"

Tom cursed. They'd found him.

He looked behind him, got painfully to his feet.

"You hear me?" The cop was standing at the perimeter of the lot, maybe twenty yards away. He looked young and jumpy, and his gun was trained on Tom's chest. "I said freeze!"

"I *am* frozen," Tom muttered.

"Now get your hands up." The cop gestured with his gun and started to advance.

Before he even realized what he was doing, Tom was running again.

"Hold it!" roared the cop. But his gun roared louder.

Tom's shoulder burned white hot. For a moment he was flying through the stinging rain. Then he was tumbling over and over on the hard wet concrete and hurting so bad he couldn't even scream. He heard a screech of brakes and came up fast against something that stopped him dead, flat on his back, staring up at the purplish, heavy night sky till the rainwater filled his eyes and he couldn't see a thing anymore.

CHAPTER THIRTEEN

No one was home at Woollard's place. Kate stood by as Stacy rapped repeatedly on the front door, but no sound of movement came from inside.

"So now what do we do?" Kate asked dismally as the rain drummed down around them. She wondered helplessly where Tom was now. She should've gone after Jasmine, got in the wagon and refused to get out. If anyone were to reach Tom and rescue him, it should be her, not that hysterical girl. And whose fault was that? Kate reflected guiltily.

"This sure is a run-down neighborhood," Stacy observed. The tenement overlooked a vacant lot on one side and some boarded-up buildings on the other. "I bet there's a lot of crime." She walked up to a cracked front window and put her elbow through it. The glass broke noisily.

"Are you crazy?" Kate demanded in disbelief.

"I prefer to think of myself as determined." Stacy reached carefully through the jagged hole she'd made and unlatched the low window. Then she climbed inside, her lithe figure soon lost to the darkness beyond.

Kate swiftly followed. It was a relief to be out of the rain, though Woollard's apartment wasn't a good deal warmer than the October night, and it reeked of whiskey and garlic.

Stacy flicked on a lamp on the desk and leafed through a whole stack of papers perched precariously on a chair.

Kate closed Woollard's dusty curtains. Spindly stems bearing withered white flowers had been pinned around the edges. Garlic flowers? "This is too weird," she muttered. "What are you looking for, Stacy?"

"Research notes, papers, tests . . ." Not finding what she wanted, Stacy impatiently swept the whole pile of papers off the chair. "Okay, then, let's think what the most likely hiding place would be."

"Takapa drove Woollard to Rico's place in his limo," Kate suggested. "So he must've picked him up someplace."

"Most likely from here," said Stacy. "Woollard lives his whole life in this place. Scared to go out."

Kate took in the crucifixes on the walls, the cryptic texts in their dusty frames and weird mystical symbols daubed about the place. "I think I'd be more scared of staying in. But okay, say they met here to talk stuff over, discuss something. . . ?"

Stacy nodded. "Or demonstrate something.

Come on, Woollard keeps his lab in this little examining room back here. . . ."

Kate followed her across the hall.

Stacy turned on the light and stared around. A low leather couch was strewn with documents, as was a long workbench along the back wall, bowing under the weight of the high-tech equipment that cluttered it. She grabbed a sheaf of papers and started flicking through them.

Kate peered at a padded envelope. "No doubt about it, Woollard's been working for Takapa." She pointed to the sender's address label on the back. "It's the address of Takapa's New Orleans hideout. I was held there for a while. He had all sorts of experiments going on." She pulled out some of the papers inside. "Cell counts . . . chromosome analysis . . ."

But Stacy was barely listening, hunched almost double over some lab results scrawled in a spidery script. "You idiot," she breathed. "You blind idiot."

Kate frowned. "Who?"

"Me. I've been taking Woollard's comments on the treated blood samples at face value—because they told me what I wanted to hear. The guy's a genius, and I just always assumed he was as committed to the work as I am. And since I don't have the equipment any more to double-check the results . . ." She laughed softly. "Oh, he's played me."

A feeling of unease twisted through Kate's insides. "What is it?"

"This research seems to run parallel to mine. Takapa must want to study Tom's genetic makeup for the same reasons I do: comparing it to other samples—like Rico's—could help identify and isolate the lupine factor."

"The werewolf gene," Kate translated. "But why would he want that? Takapa's not looking for a cure."

"No—he's been trying to stop *me* finding it." She screwed up one of the papers. "Like with the Stacy serum . . . He's treated my samples as I asked him to—but he's gone further. Altered the direction of my work without my even knowing."

"Then what does the serum actually do?"

Stacy seemed pale and sick, scanning another sheet of scrawls. "'A chronically addictive psychotropic drug . . .'" she read. "'Excitation of the adrenal gland . . .'" She looked up at Kate. "He's knocked out the pacifying effect. The serum doesn't soothe the lupine condition—it agitates it."

"So Tom's reaction was nothing to do with his particular body chemistry," Kate said slowly. "It was just the drug doing its thing."

"*Woollard* serum . . . all the time." Stacy threw down the pile of papers in despair. "But I've been running a register; I've got 'wolves out there on the street reporting back to me. They say the lupine numbers *have* gone down—and a steadily greater number of newbloods have come back for more serum; that's *fact!*" She looked at Kate desperately. "So the serum *must* be working on the lupine brain in the way it's intended—controlling newblood cravings without them having to go out and bite someone. The math works!"

But Kate was thinking about something else Stacy had read out. The report had said the serum was *chronically addictive.* And Kate remembered Swagger's tempting the gladiators to fight with a promise of *something* . . . something that was worth all that violence and pain. . . . She flicked through the contents of the envelope more carefully. "Suppose your serum works *too* well? What if taking it is *better* than going out and killing for real?" she suggested slowly.

"What do you mean?"

"I mean, what if someone's been getting new-bloods hooked on Stacy serum, the ultimate high—so they can control them through it!"

Stacy shook her head. "I haven't been able to make the stuff in that kind of volume. We weren't ready—"

"Woollard was ready," Kate said quietly, holding out a small sheaf of papers. "Top sheet's a fax from Takapa, ordering Woollard to go ahead with producing the serum in volume. It's like he's got some kind of distribution network going."

"Give me those." Stacy snatched the papers from her and scanned them. "Jesus, it's true. So I keep on handing out the drug," she added, tears in her eyes. "There's me, thinking I'm refining it—but I'm only helping Woollard make it even deadlier."

Kate nodded. "Then he turns a whole load of the stuff over to Takapa to infect *more* street kids."

Stacy put her head in her hands. "God, who knows how many 'wolves there could be hiding in this city."

"All of them more violent and aggressive than the rest of the 'wolves," Kate agreed. "And being forced to fight each other to the death."

Stacy was practically tearing her hair out. "But we still don't know *why*. Why would he build up 'wolves in such numbers and then decimate them?"

"Swagger told me that sometime soon, 'wolves would be a dime a dozen. It stands to reason that not all of the kids he turns would be fighters, so he's weeding out the weak ones."

Stacy looked at her, horrified. "You think he's breeding, what . . . a lupine militia?"

Suddenly a bloodcurdling howl sounded somewhere close by outside. Both Kate and Stacy were on their feet in an instant.

A loud crash against the front door nearly knocked it off its hinges. They heard scuffles outside. Someone started banging at the door.

"The 'wolves," Stacy whispered fearfully. "They know we're in here."

The pounding at the door grew louder and louder.

Tom woke up and wished he hadn't.

It felt like someone had taken a red-hot chisel to his left shoulder and hammered it down into the bone. He was lying curled on his side, his whole body soaked with rain and sweat. And while the ground seemed soft, he felt confined, caught in dark and cramped surroundings. He stirred and found something musty and scratchy was covering him from head to toe. An old blanket.

Memories of his ordeal seeped into his mind as he wormed his head clear of the covering. Everything was still black.

"Where am I?" he asked the darkness, afraid of what he might hear in reply.

"Quiet," muttered a voice he recognized. Jasmine. He whistled softly in relief, but then a hand pressed down over his mouth.

It was Rico, crouched down beside him. Tom guessed he must be back in the stolen station wagon. But while he might be among friends, judging from the look in Rico's dark eyes, he was nowhere near safe.

Rico pulled the blanket back over him. Tom could hear footsteps passing close by. They faltered, came closer still—then moved away.

"Jeez, that was close," said Jasmine. She emerged

awkwardly from the floor of the passenger seat, where she'd been curled up out of sight, and eased herself back behind the wheel. "Cops. Still searching the area. Tom, you okay?"

"I'll live," he muttered. "Probably. What the hell happened?"

"You got shot," said Rico, apparently impressed.

"Rookie cop," Jasmine said by way of explanation, stretching her body in the driver's seat. "You freaked him out. When he saw you were out cold, he ran to get his buddies. But we got to you first."

"We heard where to find you on the radio," Rico added.

"Bullet only nicked you," Jasmine added. "Don't think it's too bad."

"Neither is this dressing," Tom realized, pressing gingerly at the clean bandages binding his shoulder. "Thanks."

Rico shrugged. "Took 'em from the drugstore. Jasmine taped you up. Just like she used to tape up Ramon when he been fighting."

Jasmine turned away. "Shut your mouth, Rico," she snapped, but Tom heard the tremble in her voice.

"You was always good to him, Jas. . . ."

Tom saw the pain in Rico's face, the tears welling in his black eyes. He put a hand on his shoulder. "I'm so sorry, Rico."

"Ain't going to cry," Rico said fiercely, brushing

Tom's hand away, his breath growing hoarse and ragged. "Going to get even. Right, Jas?"

"You know it," she said. "Now, be good. Take your inhaler."

"It don't work," he complained.

"Do it," Jasmine snapped. "You going to keel over before you get even with that mad bitch who did Ramon?"

His young, clear face still screwed up with emotion, Rico took two wheezy puffs on his inhaler.

"Thanks for coming after me," Tom said. "Thank you both."

"Forget it," Jasmine said distantly. "With the guys gone, Polar turned 'wolf, and Ramon . . . Well. Guess we got to look after the friends we got left." She started the wagon's engine. "And that means getting you to a doctor. Patched you up the best I could, but Woollard should take a look. He's got some pills; they'll help with the pain."

"But he lied to us about Stacy wanting my blood," said Rico, rubbing his forearm.

"I'm not sure we can trust him," Tom agreed, "and neither is the man I met tonight."

Jasmine cut the engine, looked at him gravely. "The real Jicaque, right?"

"Right." He winced as he tried to straighten his shoulder.

Jasmine sighed heavily. "Well, then, I guess we get Stacy Stein to take a look."

"And hook up with Kate," Tom added automatically.

"Don't worry, Tommy." She pulled out into the dark, silent street. "I ain't forgotten Kate."

Kate turned to Stacy as the banging on the front door grew louder. "There must be a back way out of here."

Stacy nodded. "Let's find it."

But as they reached the hall, they heard a frantic voice at the door rise above the banging: "Stacy! I know you're in there—I saw your car outside. Let me in! He'll get me! Can't find my keys, let me in!"

"That's Woollard," Stacy breathed, heading for the front door. "He sounds terrified."

Kate hung back in the hallway as Stacy fumbled with the door locks and finally got the door open.

Woollard shambled in on his knees, clutching his stomach, and pitched forward.

"Stacy," he gasped. "How'd you get in here? Close the door, for God's sake."

Stacy tried, but Woollard's legs were blocking the way. "Help me, Kate!" she said.

Kate took the doctor by his clammy hands and dragged him forward. To her horror she found he was leaving a thick trail of blood in his wake.

While Stacy locked the door and slammed the bolts home, Kate turned Woollard over gently. A large wound had been gouged in his stomach.

"Knife." He stared up at her with clouded eyes. "Hurts. Get me a drink."

She looked down at him and shook her head. "We know what you've been doing. We know you've been working for Takapa!"

He nodded and clutched at Kate's wrist with sticky red fingers. "Takapa," he rasped. "Got all he can from me. I've made his dreams come true."

"What are you talking about?" Stacy said, coming to join them.

"Mass production." Woollard smiled bleakly. "Add just a single drop of Stacy serum to a test tube of ordinary blood plasma. . . . In under an hour the blood is pure serum. Ready to go to work on another poor 'wolf junkie . . ."

Kate pulled her wrist away in disgust, and Woollard winced.

"The serum is now as addictive as it can be," he croaked. "So Takapa thinks it's high time I was turned 'wolf too." Woollard gave a weak, mirthless laugh that turned into a cough. Blood appeared on his lips. "It was the threat of that hanging over me that made me work for him in the first place."

Kate looked down at him helplessly. "Takapa did this to you?"

Woollard feebly shook his head. "Still out there," he murmured, wide-eyed. "Tried to run, but—"

Suddenly there was a glassy crash from the living room. Before Kate or Stacy could react, the light snapped on and a large shadow fell over them.

"Oh, Jesus." Kate shut her eyes, felt a terrible cold take her body. "Please, no."

Swagger stood towering over them. He must've ignored the bolted door and simply come in through the window as they had. His eyes were bloodshot and wild; his wide, crusty mouth hung open in a vicious grin. A vivid gash ran across his forehead, clumsily stitched; the sutures looked like black flies feeding on the wound.

"Well, well," he said, glancing between Kate and Stacy. "Look who we got here."

"Don't hurt me any more," Woollard begged feebly. "Please."

"You could've been something, Doc," Swagger told him. "Could've stood beside Takapa and me and welcomed in the new world. All you needed was guts, old man." He giggled. "Guess they fell out through that hole in your belly, right?"

Kate stared across at Stacy in dismay. Swagger was looking spaced out, euphoric, like Tom had looked on the bridge. "He's taken the serum," she hissed.

"Right," Swagger agreed, "and I'm in the mood to party."

Kate gasped as he hauled her up by her hair.

"Liked you better with black hair, sweetheart," he slurred. "But it was sweet of you to make the effort for ol' Swag." She tried to struggle free, but when he held the switchblade to her throat, still wet with Woollard's blood, she stayed very, very still.

"Now get into the examination room, Stein," he snarled. "Or this little honey here's gonna be gargling blood."

Kate held her breath. She could smell the rank odor of his sweat saturating his clothes. He kept shifting his weight from foot to foot, like he couldn't hold still. The blade pressed harder against her neck as he marched her inside the examination room after Stacy.

"I need every piece of paper out of this hole," Swagger told her. "Takapa wants all his research back. You got brains; pick it all out for me."

Stacy nodded, cowed and pale, and started to collect the scattered papers. Outside, Woollard was moaning softly in the hallway.

"Shame you had to find out about this, Stein," Swagger snarled. "Takapa likes you. You been good to us."

"You tricked me," she said quietly.

"We would have gone on tricking you, too. Used you a whole lot more and then given you the bite like your old man. But Takapa saw you watching when he was outside Ramon's with the doc tonight. Guess he could see the way the cookie crumbled way across the street." He giggled again. "He said you'd work it out."

Stacy finished collecting the papers and held them out to him.

He put the knife away to take them. Kate let out a shuddering sigh of relief.

"Now let her go," said Stacy, trying to sound brave. And failing.

"Nuh-uh," said Swagger. "Anyway, not your problem. 'Cause now you have to die."

Stacy stared at him, speechless for a second, before his big fist crashed into her chin and sent her reeling back over the couch, where she lay still.

"No!" shouted Kate, but he tightened his grip around her throat, choking her off.

"Cold out tonight, ain't it?" Swagger laughed. "Still, a little fire will warm us all up."

Struggling and writhing in his grip, Kate was dragged out of the room. She saw Woollard rocking feebly on his back like an overturned tortoise.

"You're going nowhere, gutless," Swagger shouted, pulling Kate into the living room. "So, babe. Just you and me now, huh? Where's your freak boyfriend?" He put the papers in his coat pocket. "I want to have some fun with him."

"He's . . . he's left," she croaked. "Gone."

"Like I believe you," he said, pulling a cigarette lighter from his pocket. "But if that bastard *has* skipped town, I hope he said 'bye to his folks first. 'Cause Marcie's going to make sure he won't get the chance again."

"Where is she?" Kate asked fearfully.

"Yakking with Takapa." Swagger held the oily

flame up close to her cheek, and she flinched. "But later, when it's nice and quiet, she's going to visit Tom's mommy and daddy and . . ."

Kate gasped as he held the lighter flame to the thick curtains. The heavy fabric smoldered for a few seconds, then caught fire. He crossed the room, starting more little fires here and there until the room was filled with dark smoke and flames.

"Once a fire takes hold of one of these old places . . ." Swagger whistled. "They'll be using dental records to tell Woollard and Stein apart."

"No!" Kate cried again. She'd never felt more helpless as Swagger kicked the last glinting glass teeth from the window frame and carried her out through it. The cold night air fanned the flames, and soon smoke was billowing out through the broken window.

"You can't do this," Kate sobbed, praying someone would pass by and see the flames, go for help. But the street was quiet; only Polar stood by, silent as ever, leaning against a black car and viewing the spectacle through his camera. "Swagger," she tried again. "For God's sake, let them go."

"Nuh-uh." He shoved her toward the car, and Polar turned and opened the rear door for her. "Oh, and by the way." Swagger hissed wetly in her ear. "You'll be begging me to let *you* burn when you find out what I got lined up for you."

CHAPTER FOURTEEN

Tom saw the smoke the second they rounded the corner into Woollard's street. "That's Woollard's place! Come on!"

"Firefighters are going to be here soon," Jasmine warned him. "The cops, everyone."

"Then we'd better be fast!" Tom yelled at her. "We don't know who's trapped in there!"

Cursing under her breath, Jasmine stamped on the gas and they accelerated down the street.

Tom berated himself for not having agreed to come straight here. He'd thought it safest if they all confronted Woollard together and assumed that Stacy and Kate would be waiting at Ramon's. But they'd already taken off from there. Kate had left a brief note that confirmed the worst:

> *Tom—If you're not okay, I'll kill you. ;-) Gone to see Woollard.*
>
> K

Just like her: she'd leave him a scribbled emoticon but never so much as an *x*. Jasmine had found him some painkillers, and then they'd headed over to Woollard's.

And found an inferno.

Jasmine hit the brakes and the wagon skidded to a halt on the wet street. Tom jumped out, looked at her expectantly.

"I'll stay here," she announced, "and you'd better be quick. When the cops come calling, we're out of here." Her pretty face softened. "Don't take any risks you don't have to," she added quietly. "Okay?"

"Okay," Tom told her solemnly. "Rico, you'd better stay here too."

Rico said something loud and probably very offensive in Spanish and leapt from the wagon to join him.

A few night-owl neighbors across the street were staring in wonder from their windows, but Tom didn't care who saw him now. "Kate!" he yelled. "Kate, are you in there?"

"Back way," said Rico, racing toward the vacant lot next to the house. "Fire might not have reached there yet."

Tom chased after him.

Rico was right. The flames hadn't yet reached this part of the building. The wood of the back door was slimy with mold. He thought of all Woollard's locks and bolts and mystical protections to keep the dark things out—yet the shell of his apartment was so old and worn it wouldn't keep out a determined mouse.

With a couple of well-placed kicks Tom booted open the door. Black smoke boiled out in his face. He recoiled, coughing and spluttering.

"Better leave this to me, Tom," said Rico. "If you turn howler in there, you going to burn your fur."

And with that, Rico rushed inside.

"Come back!" Tom yelled, his eyes streaming. "Rico!"

There was no reply. Tom dashed in after him, found himself in Woollard's kitchen. He yanked the yellow curtains down from the windows and soaked them in the sink. Then, crouching down low where the smoke was less dense, he draped the wet curtains over his head and pressed on through to the passageway.

Woollard's body lay prone outside the living room. Tom felt his neck for a pulse.

So much for answers. He was dead.

Tom peered into the living room. The fire was fiercest here. The arcane texts that papered the walls, the charms, the feeble garlic flowers, all were blackening to a charred mass. Glass cracked as a heavy frame tumbled from the wall to land at Tom's feet. He saw it held Woollard's doctorate, hard-won in a brighter time.

"Tom!"

His heart leapt; that was Stacy's voice, from across the passageway. Tom crawled from the room, the damp fabric heavy about his head and injured shoulder. He placed the doctorate beside Woollard's corpse as he passed by.

He squinted into the smoky room. Suddenly Stacy came into view, coughing, eyes streaming. Rico appeared just behind her.

"I woke her up!" he wheezed in triumph.

"Where's Kate?" Tom asked Stacy, handing her the other soaked curtain.

She took it and wrapped it around herself and Rico. "Swagger took her."

Tom stared at Stacy blankly, the flames and smoke suddenly nothing to him.

"We have to get out!" she shouted, grabbing Tom's arm.

Tom gasped at the wrench on his injured shoulder. The pain was enough to snap him out of his despair, sparking his resolve. He swiftly led the way back outside, where they all three gulped down icy sharp breaths of the damp night air.

"Got your inhaler, Rico?" Tom asked.

The boy coughed thickly and nodded.

A distant wailing reached them over the gloating roar of the flames as they consumed more and more of the apartment. Sirens.

"We may not want it, but here it comes," said Tom huskily. "Let's get out of here." He led the charge back around to the front of the building to where Jasmine waited.

The streets in the neighborhood were crawling by now with fire trucks, cop cars, and ambulances, blue lights blinding the night, sirens screaming past.

"Close," Jasmine remarked when they stopped at the next light. She was half smiling at Tom, her dark eyes suggesting approval.

"Too close," he agreed. "But we were too late to help Kate." He felt sick inside and utterly helpless.

"You shoulda seen it in there, Jas," Rico chirped from the backseat.

"Rico was fantastic," Stacy said with feeling. "Dragged me off the couch and onto the floor, where there was less smoke. Helped bring me around."

Rico shrugged. "Wasn't nothing."

"Okay, heroes!" Jasmine called. "Where the hell am I driving?"

"To the ice arena, I guess," Tom said grimly. "That's where Swagger will be. And Kate."

"I'd better tell you what the hell happened in there," said Stacy.

Tom's heart sank like a rock as he heard how Kate had been dragged away. "So Takapa's back in New York, and Marcie's come to join him. Whatever his plans are, they must be close to coming together."

188

"Midnight, Friday," Jasmine recalled. "Swagger said he wanted us all to check his skating rink at midnight on Friday to swear allegiance or whatever."

"Something must be going down," Stacy agreed, checking her watch. "And we're four hours into Friday already."

"I don't care about Takapa." Rico spoke up. "What about Kate?"

"My thoughts exactly," muttered Tom.

"You think Swagger . . . ?" Jasmine sounded kind of awkward for once. "Well—do you think he'll have killed her?"

"I don't think so," said Tom, praying he was right. "Otherwise, why not kill her at Woollard's? And both Marcie and Takapa want her pretty bad."

"This Takapa's a son of a bitch," Stacy said. "From what Kate has seen, it looks like he's breeding his own militia."

"Nice thought." Tom shook his head. "Just imagine. Kids off the street, all the flotsam and jetsam of a city . . . trained like soldiers to fight and to kill but with the strength, the speed, and the senses of a werewolf."

"I don't want to imagine that," muttered Jasmine with a shiver.

"And all hooked on a drug so addictive they'll follow any command to get it." Stacy sighed. "Thanks to me: dumbest genius on the East Coast."

"I met dumber," Rico piped up matter-of-factly.

"Oh God." Stacy clapped both hands to her face. "I just remembered. I was so out of it, I can't be sure, but . . ."

Tom frowned. "What?"

"Swagger. I heard him say, Tom, after he'd hit me . . ." She looked at him and bit her lip. "I heard him say Marcie Folan was going after your parents—later tonight."

Tom felt his world fall away. He tried to speak, but the words withered up at the back of his throat. "That evil bitch," he managed to croak. "She's taken so much. . . ."

"Well, I've taken a whole bellyful of *her*," said Jasmine fiercely, rounding a corner. "She ain't hurting nobody else."

"We know where his mom and dad are," chirped Rico. "It was on the cop radio. First Western Hotel, over on Madison, room 3003. We could go get them. Pick them up."

"And do what?" Tom said bitterly. "Tell them their son's a werewolf? And that the woman they think is another poor grieving parent is actually planning to tear them apart?" His voice was rising higher. "You think they'll buy all that? Sure! 'Oh, sorry, son, we thought you were just a murderer, not the freaking wolfman. . . .'"

Jasmine placed her hand on his arm. "Okay. Enough, Tom."

Tom massaged his temples. He felt exhausted,

and his shoulder was still throbbing, setting his whole spine on edge. "I'm sorry," he muttered.

"It's okay," Rico told him. "I know you ain't mad at me."

"We need a proper plan," said Stacy. "We need to think about this." She shut her eyes, started muttering to herself.

Rico watched her, intrigued.

"That brainy stuff might work, sure," said Jasmine quietly, seriously, as she pulled up at the next set of lights. "But seems to me you have to fight fire with fire." She shot Tom a dark look. "Know what I'm saying?" She held open her jacket. Protruding from her jeans pocket, glistening black, was the handle of Ramon's gun.

Tom stared at it, dark against the creamy brown skin of Jasmine's midriff.

"I've got an idea," Stacy announced.

Jasmine let her jacket hang back down, hiding both the gun and her bare flesh from sight. "So do I," she murmured, her eyes wide and maybe just a little scared, holding Tom's.

The ice arena looked no more appealing by starlight than in the cold, gray light of yesterday's dawn. To Kate its squat, rounded shape gave it the silhouette of some giant black beetle hunched over the land.

Swagger was half dragging, half carrying her

through the rubble-strewn parking lot, away from the main entrance. "We're taking the back way," he informed Polar, who followed mutely behind. "Hell, will you dump that camera, man? You look like a retard."

Polar reluctantly lowered the camera.

"You could pick up some tips from Polar, Swagger. You'd look a whole lot cuter if we couldn't see your face," Kate goaded him. "And why are we skulking into your sleaze palace the back way?"

"I don't want no one seeing you come in," he told her. "'Cause no one is going to see you come out again." He passed Polar a key to open the heavy padlock on a set of moldering fire doors. Then Swagger yanked them open and forced Kate inside.

They were in the arena's cavernous locker rooms. The stench was worse than the last time she'd been here: sweat and urine and stuff she'd rather not dwell on. She soon learned the reason why.

The place had been converted into a kind of holding area. All around, people were gathered in groups, slumped on the floor or against cracked tile walls. Their eyes were glazed. They were being held in crude pens fashioned from welded fenders, girders, bits of scrap iron—presumably anything Swagger's thugs could lay their hands on. A bucket made do for a toilet. The damp concrete floor was their table, littered with assorted fast-food debris: empty buckets of chicken, burger wrappers, soda cans.

It was like a detention camp for all the poor souls Swagger and his kind had snatched from the streets.

Polar stood beside Kate, looking down at his scruffy sneakers as if trying to blank out the rest of his surroundings.

"Why are you keeping these people here like this, Swagger?" she demanded.

"They won't be here long. Arrived last night. Winners of the national heats, shipped in from all over the country." He tightened his viselike grip on the back of her neck. "My gladiators. Ready for the big rumble. Midnight tonight."

Kate shivered. "That's when you wanted Ramon's gang to come here."

"That was the plan." He grinned and clapped Polar on the back. "I like my troops to be well fed before battle."

"So anyone who won't take the bite becomes the pre-match snack, is that it?" She glared at Polar beside her. "And I guess *you* decided you'd rather chow down yourself than be part of the meal." Then she paused as the full significance of Swagger's words sank in. "Troops? Gladiators?"

Swagger leaned in close, nuzzled his big greasy nose into her ear. "They're here to prove themselves, see? Only the strongest, the fiercest, have a place in Takapa's private army. He's been recruiting in a dozen states, and the big face-off is right here—with

193

me presiding. This is where we build the real crack force, right here, in New York. . . ."

"Crack force?" Kate snorted. "Crackheads, more like."

Swagger was oblivious to her scorn. He spun her around to face him. "They'll fight for me, *die* for me."

"Not for you," Kate argued. "For the drug you tricked Stacy into creating. Once they're hooked on that, they'll do anything for a fix."

"That's right. And only the strongest will live." His eyes shone as he stared into the distance, and Kate was glad she couldn't see what he was seeing. "We have to make fighters out of this scum, have to make them the best. So we have to *keep* them fighting, see? Make them faster, sharper, meaner. Strip out the weak till we got an unbeatable army, ready and waiting . . ."

Without warning he snatched the camera from Polar's hands. The carry strap snapped and Polar gave a weird, high-pitched squeal, like he'd lost a piece of himself. Swagger opened a locker, tossed the camera inside, and turned the little key in the lock. Then he threw it into one of the pens.

"You're watching *her* now," Swagger told him. "With your own eyes, not through a lens. Retard."

Polar slumped his shoulders and slowly nodded.

Some of the people in this makeshift slammer were roused by the clang of the locker door slamming.

"You bringing us the stuff?" a man called, and

one by one the others began to rise and take up the call. Some even got to their feet, hanging from the rusty bars of their cells, first angry, but soon pleading and pathetic. All clamoring for their fix.

"They can shout all they want." Swagger shoved Kate out of the locker room into a grimy reception area. "But they'll just have to wait. When they wait, the kick's even better . . . and the fighting's so much sweeter."

Kate massaged the back of her neck, turned to face him. "You're sick."

Swagger dropped his voice to a stage whisper. "You might want to keep quiet now." He turned to Polar. "Watch her." Then he disappeared around a corner.

Kate heard him knock on a door.

"Well?" came an imperious voice, a hint of something European in the accent. Kate recognized it at once, and it chilled her. Takapa.

She heard Swagger open the door and go inside. This was it, then. Takapa would come out of his office now and find her. She glanced at Polar. He was looking back toward the locker room, thinking about his camera, no doubt. If she could catch him off guard . . .

She took a slow step toward him, but he caught the movement, whirled back around, and shook his head.

"Stein and Woollard are dead," she heard Swagger

announce. "I burned 'em, along with any remaining evidence."

Now Kate heard the rustling of papers.

"Ah, my documents," purred Takapa. "Invaluable research. The fruits of which will transform human society." He paused. "With Stein dead you can get the remaining serum from her offices at the hospital. Our fighters will need it."

"Already arranged," Swagger reported. "Kes is dealing with that now. Serum supplies to be dished up at eighteen hundred hours."

Takapa sounded amused. "Not too much, mind. Then we'll leave them to simmer for six hours. Their aggression levels will remain high and their cravings will be at their most extreme. Excellent, Swagger." His voice suddenly hardened. "Now, have you found the wereling and the Folan girl?"

Kate shut her eyes, held her breath.

"Not yet," said Swagger. "But I got people working on it. I'm expecting news soon."

A reprieve? Why was Swagger risking his own life with a lie that size? Kate bit her lip, more scared now than ever. There could only be one reason.

Swagger had his own plans for her.

"Marcie Folan is resting now in my suite," Takapa said. "If the wereling isn't found, she intends to inflict damage on his parents at dawn to draw him back out into the open."

"I know that. She told me herself, coming back from Gun Hill."

"It would be . . . good public relations if we could spare her the risk and the bother and find him first."

Kate looked imploringly at Polar, his face a dark shadow beneath his hood. "Let me go," she mouthed. "Let me warn them!"

He didn't move.

"Make no mistake, we still want the wereling, Swagger. We need him." Takapa paused. "And *I* want the girl. Her own contribution will be sweet indeed."

"Understood, sir. If she's still in the city, we'll find her."

Kate heard Swagger's heavy footsteps before the door closed behind him. A second later he was back, his gargoyle grin large on his heavy face. "Why, here you are now!" he whispered. "Ain't that a surprise."

Kate took a shuddering breath. "What are you going to do with me?"

He just smiled and took another step closer.

CHAPTER FIFTEEN

"Coast's clear," whispered Jasmine.

Tom followed her stealthily across the hotel lobby. It was 5:30 a.m. The night receptionist was on the phone, her long hair hanging down over her face. She didn't notice them tiptoe into the large elevator. Tom held his breath until the heavy brass doors closed and their upward journey was under way. His palms were slick with sweat, but his mouth was dry.

Jasmine was staring into space, cool, placid, and serene. Like she planned this kind of thing every day.

Stacy had come up with a good plan. But no matter how clever, it was another stopgap measure; more time spent hiding in the dark till the bogeyman went away. And Marcie Folan wasn't going away anytime soon—unless they made her.

As the elevator crawled up to the thirtieth floor, Tom had never felt so alone. No one but Rico even knew they were here.

He sorted through the night's feverish memories.

"Here's what we do," Stacy had announced in the back of the wagon. "I'm a virologist. So, if we get Tom's parents to the hospital, I can fake an outbreak of something nasty and highly contagious and have them placed in isolation. That way *no one* can get to them."

"But your colleagues, other medical staff," Tom argued. "They'd question your diagnosis the second they looked at them."

"Careful management, Tom. Blind eyes and sympathetic ears," Stacy said. "If I call on the right people, we can have your mom and dad transferred to another hospital out of state, no questions asked."

"You going tell his *mami* and *papi* about the howlers?" Rico was wide-eyed. "They'll be locking *you* up for being crazy."

"All they need to know for now is that Tom's okay, that he's not a murderer, but that their own lives are in danger." She looked at Tom. "I'll leave you to explain to them what else you feel you can."

"I can't see them." Tom shook his head. "Can't face them. Not until this is over. Not until—" He broke off, swallowing back the threatening tears. "Damn, where's Jicaque? He's supposed to be helping us . . . and what's happening to Kate?"

"One thing at a time, Tom." Stacy put a comforting hand on his shoulder. "And if Jicaque's all you say he is, he'll come through for you."

199

We'll see, Tom thought.

He had written a note to his parents on the back of a postcard, telling them to go to Park East Hospital and ask for Stacy and not to tell Marcie or Hal Folan where they'd gone. Never to speak to them again. Asking them to trust him.

Once Jasmine had dropped Stacy at the hospital to make the necessary arrangements, they'd driven over to the First Western. They'd sent in Rico on a commando-style mission to slide the postcard under the Andersons' door.

Then they'd waited.

Tom's heart had lurched in his chest when he saw his mom and dad emerge from the hotel ten minutes later. They jumped in the back of a yellow cab and drove away. "We did it," he breathed. "Marcie can't get them."

"For now," Jasmine added. "I don't have no mom or dad, Tom. But I want you to hang on to yours." She tapped her hip where the gun was hidden. "Let's go. Rico, wait in the car."

"Aw, Jas," Rico complained. But she gave him a stern look. He made a face and nodded reluctantly.

Quickly, quietly, Tom and Jasmine walked toward the hotel's reception. . . .

Ping.

The elevator's electronic chime jarred Tom from his memories. They had reached the thirtieth floor.

"Let's finish this," muttered Jasmine.

The corridor was quiet. Jasmine soon picked the lock on room 3003, and Tom followed her inside.

The moment he breathed in the still-lingering smell of his dad's deodorant, a wave of almost unbearable homesickness overcame him. His mom's clothes lay strewn on a chair. The same suitcases they'd taken to Seattle, where the whole nightmare had begun, were stowed beside the TV in a corner of the room.

Tom felt hot and flushed and opened the window a fraction. Then he sat heavily on the king-sized bed.

Jasmine joined him, saying nothing. She took the gun from her pocket and turned it around in her hands.

"You ever use that on someone?" he asked.

"You kidding me?" She shot him a dark look. "How's that shoulder of yours?"

"Hurts like hell."

"Just a scratch, Tommy. Just a scratch. You ever seen someone shot dead?" Jasmine's voice trembled a fraction. "I did once. This guy I knew? He was shot in the guts. . . . He was kind of crazy, but he had this great smile, you know. . . ." She sighed softly. "So much blood when he got shot. Everywhere. We couldn't stop it. We watched him die for hours and hours, too scared to do jack shit, too scared to go to the cops. . . ."

"Who shot him?" Tom murmured.

"The guy's best friend," said Jasmine, weighing the gun in her hand. "They ripped off some gas station, got really high. Tried to split the cash between them, but they couldn't count straight . . . started fighting over a ten-dollar bill or something." Her voice was drained of all emotion. "And this guy I knew with the cute smile . . . he lost the fight. His whole life just bled out of him over this dumbass ten bucks. 'Cause his dumbass friend had a gun like this one, loaded and ready to go." She looked at him. "Kind of a waste, don't you think?"

Tom just nodded dumbly.

Jasmine kept talking, her voice dull like the sheen on the black metal of the gun barrel. "Looks kind of cool, don't it? In the movies and stuff, I mean. And these punks, they think all they got to do is pick up a gun and suddenly they're a real man. Puff got ahold of this one. Got it from some guy over in Queens . . ." She passed it to Tom. "Don't look like so much, does it? But one shot from this and . . ."

He looked at her. "Murder?"

She shook her head, and when she spoke again, she sounded fiercer than he'd ever heard her. "Not if you use it against this Marcie bitch," she said. "That bitch who killed Ramon. That bitch who thinks she's going to kill your parents here tonight." She pointed at the gun. "This ain't a murder. It's an execution."

"An execution," he echoed. "I guess . . . I guess I should do it." He still felt the tingling traces of Stacy's serum in his veins. Was that why he was going along with this? A few months ago just holding a gun would've freaked him out. Now he found himself lifting the gun, aiming it at the door, curling his finger around the trigger, picturing Marcie coming into range. . . .

Jasmine had picked up a picture from the bedside table. Mom's side, he guessed.

"Look at you," she murmured. "And who's the cute kid?"

"My brother, Joe."

"He ain't staying here?"

"Guess he's at Aunt Rachel's or something." Tom wiped wetness from his eyes.

Jasmine put the photo back on the table, shifted a fraction closer to him. "You must miss your family real bad."

"I do."

"Never had much family myself . . . Hanging with Ramon, Puff, Cicero, Rico . . . That was my family."

Tom nodded. "And the 'wolves ruined everything."

"For the both of us." She slapped her hand down on his. "But hey, we're still standing, right? Or sitting, anyway."

She wasn't moving her hand away. It was cool and reassuring on top of his own.

"I guess you just have to get through stuff in life," Tom ventured. "You have to adapt, you know?"

"Oh yeah. I know all about adapting." She looked at him with an intensity that made his skin tingle. "First time I met you, I thought you were, well, kind of a pussy. Then I thought you were the big, bad 'wolf, a howler spy or something. But I've been watching you, Tommy. Stuff you've done. The way you handle yourself." Her fingertips were caressing the rough skin on his knuckles. "And I want you to know, I'm impressed."

He shrugged. "I've been lucky, that's all."

She laughed softly. "Boy, you don't know what lucky is." She leaned in closer to him, angled her face toward his. "Do you want to know?"

Then she pressed her mouth against his.

Tom felt a light flick of her tongue, found himself responding. Suddenly they were caught up in a hot, wet kiss. Tom's thoughts were scattered and lost. All he could feel was the heat of the kiss buzzing through him, the sweet smell of Jasmine's sweat, the taste of her tongue snaking around inside his mouth. He went to slide his arms around her—and felt the gun, cold and heavy in his right hand.

He jumped away like a shock had bolted through him.

Jasmine stared at him, scared and vulnerable. "What? What'd I do?"

"I can't do this," he muttered.

In a blink the old, hard look was back, set on her face like a mask. "What, you suddenly got religion or something?"

"This isn't who I want to be," he said. The gun weighed heavy in his hand. "The guy you think I am, the stuff you like about me . . . That's the stuff I hate."

"Sure," she said. "I guess that's why you hang with Kate. Nice, clean, smart shoulder to cry on, huh?"

"No, it's not that," he protested. "I . . . I'm sorry." He turned away, placed the gun on the dresser.

"You having second thoughts about that too?"

He closed his eyes. "I know it's the only way to be free of Marcie and Takapa. To protect the people I love."

"Like Kate?" Jasmine said quietly.

Tom didn't answer her.

He heard Jasmine rise up from the bed and walk to the door. "I'll be waiting outside with Rico," she announced, her tone as cold as the night air gusting in through the window. "When she comes in . . . just don't miss."

The door clicked shut behind her.

Tom sat on the bed, one hand on a little pile of his parents' clothes, one on the gun. He registered that the sky was starting to lighten, but his attention was fixed wholly on the closed door. The minutes stretched by. His shoulder ached. A part of him ached for Jasmine to come back. To feel someone beside him, to help him do this thing he knew he—

There was a scratching, scraping sound at the lock.

Tom jumped up from the bed.

The doorknob was turning, very slightly, very slowly.

He held the gun in both hands and aimed it at the door.

The door jumped a fraction as the catch released.

Tom held his breath. Gritted his teeth. Checked his grip on the gun. Felt his world start to tilt as the door swung open, slowly, so slowly. . . .

The dim light of the breaking dawn was enough to cast only the faintest of shadows. But Tom still caught the movement behind him.

He whirled around. Someone big and ugly was standing behind him, his fist swinging toward Tom's face.

Then the world jarred into blackness.

For Kate the hours were passing slowly and uncomfortably in claustrophobic darkness. Swagger had forced her inside a cramped locker. There was no room to move, and her long legs were buzzing with pins and needles. It was hard to breathe; she had to sit with her mouth pressed up against the grille in the narrow door, snatching gasps of the foul-smelling air. Her muscles ached with inaction, and she had to fight the panic that kept threatening to overwhelm her. What was he planning for her?

"Better keep quiet," Swagger had said as he'd squeezed her inside. "If you start screaming, remember, your mom's right across the hall."

It was impossible to tell how much time had passed. She'd been stuffed inside the locker around seven in the morning and left for what felt like forever. Swagger, or one of his men, had allowed her out twice for a few minutes' "exercise." What a joke. By the time she'd finished flailing about on the damp floor, trying to ease the cramps in her arms and legs, they were ready to bundle her back inside. Her back throbbed with pain, her head was splitting; this was torture, pure and simple, but she was damned if she would let Swagger see how much she hurt.

What was he going to do to her? Was this just some sadistic payback before he handed her over to Takapa? Or was he planning to kill her himself? The cold thoughts rolled around till her whole head felt bruised.

Six o'clock in the evening had rolled around at last; she knew because Kes and the rest of Swagger's mangy generals had come to distribute little tubes of serum—taken from Stacy's labs, she guessed.

In her darkest moments Kate wished she'd been

left behind in the blaze at Woollard's place—anything would be better than being trapped here in the dark, waiting for the end to come. But as she heard the gladiators moaning and screaming and fighting for their meager fix of the drug, she found herself counting her lucky stars that she wasn't among them.

Near midnight she saw Polar creeping cautiously into her narrow field of vision. "Please," she whispered. "Let me out, Polar. Just for a minute. *Please!*"

He hadn't come to see her. He was pulling at the lockers lining the adjacent wall. Of course, looking for his camera. But Swagger had thrown away the key. . . .

"Hey! Kid!" Kate squinted through the rusting grille. A skinny woman was beckoning to Polar from one of the makeshift pens. Her bleached hair was greasy and matted, her eyes bruised and blue, and she was forcing a crooked smile. "I think I got what you need."

Polar turned to face the woman. She was tapping a tiny key against the bars of her cage. Polar immediately rushed over to get it.

But the woman snatched her hand away. "What are you going to give me in return, sugar?" She smiled like she was trying to flirt, but it came out like a grimace. "Got some more stuff? We need some . . . just a little. You know you got it. . . ."

Kate saw the woman's companions in the cage feign careful disinterest in what was happening. Saw them pass looks and shift subtly into crouching positions. "It's a trick, Polar!" she yelled. If she could get some favor with him, maybe—

But her warning came too late. He had reached into the pen to take the key, and one of the men had grabbed his arm. Polar was yanked forward and his head crashed against one of the cell bars. While he was held up against the door of the pen, helpless, the other men searched his pockets.

"He doesn't have any!" shouted a man in ragged clothes. He turned on the bleached-blond woman. "You said he'd have some."

"How was I supposed to know?" she yelled back at him.

"We can hold him here," said an Asian guy, "and threaten to kill him if we don't get more!"

Someone else in another cell started up. "If you're getting some, *we* should get some!"

Soon the call was taken up by countless others. The noise boomed through the cavernous room, making Kate's locker vibrate and rattle. She shut her eyes, clasping her hands over her ears.

"All right, simmer down!" Swagger looked like he'd come hoping for trouble. "What is this?"

"We want more stuff!" snarled the Asian guy.

"We'll kill your buddy here!" added the guy in the ragged clothes.

Swagger sneered around at his prisoners. "You get nothing more till you earn it."

The blond woman yanked Polar back against the bars. His head struck the metal with a weirdly melodious chime. "We mean it!" she said, shaking, almost frothing at the mouth.

Kate watched the big man make a show of thinking about it. At last he spoke.

"Kill him. I don't need him."

He turned and strutted over to Kate's locker, ignoring the clamor that greeted his words.

She shrank back from the grille, but there was nowhere to go.

He winked at her. "Enjoy the show."

As he moved aside, she caught a glimpse of Polar, still pinned helplessly against the bars, while the blonde and her cellmates beat his body like a punching bag, egged on by the other prisoners, screaming out their frustration and rage.

She waited for Polar to transform, to let loose his 'wolf. But maybe they'd hit him too hard, too quick. He only broke his silence with a long, loud scream of despair that twisted her guts.

Kate turned away, shaking uncontrollably. How long now before she was thrown to these animals herself?

Chapter Sixteen

When Tom became aware of the world again, he was tied to a chair in a dingy office. Fatigue defined every muscle in his body.

Behind the desk in front of him was a pink-eyed, skinny man in a dark suit that emphasized his ghostly complexion. A silver helix earring snaked down from his only ear. His skin was cratered with acne scars, and his white hair speckled out of his flaking scalp. He bared his sharp yellow teeth in a knowing grin.

"Takapa?" Tom croaked.

The man nodded. "Here we are, face-to-face at last. You've been a tiresome drain on my resources, Tom Anderson. Thank you for allowing yourself to be captured so easily."

"How did that guy get in through a window thirty stories up?" Tom muttered.

"The platform used by the hotel window cleaners," Takapa said. "That's why Marcie booked that particular room on the Andersons' behalf."

Tom felt disgusted with himself. "I didn't check the window," he said.

"He and Marcie took you out of there in the same way so as not to arouse suspicion. But come now." Takapa rose from his chair. His suit hung baggily from his skeletal frame. "I think you're relieved in a way, aren't you? I don't believe you're a killer, Tom." He smiled down at his captive, his watery eyes gleaming. "I believe that if Marcie or I had walked through that door, you could not have brought yourself to shoot."

Tom flashed a big, fake smile back up at him. "If you're that curious, how about we stage a reconstruction?"

"Then you'll be needing me." The door swung open and Marcie Folan walked in. Like Takapa, she smiled down at him gloatingly, her skin taut over her cheekbones.

Tom felt a jolt of pure fear. Maybe he should try to bring on the change, try to escape. But he knew he was faced now by real adepts. They could change faster than he could, and against the two of them he wouldn't stand a chance.

"Forgive my intrusion," Marcie went on. "Say, Tom, how about we take the reconstruction back a step further—where are your parents?"

Tom looked away. "Where you'll never find them."

"Are you sure? You know how persistent I can be." She took hold of his bruised chin and forced him to look at her. "And where is my daughter?"

He frowned, a spark of hope stirring somewhere inside. "I thought *you* had her."

"Did you indeed?" Marcie murmured, her blue eyes boring into him, trying to read his thoughts. "Takapa, I do believe he's telling the truth."

"We'll find her." With his pink eyes, short white hair, and long narrow face, there was the look of a lab rat about Takapa. "In the meantime, after the fun tonight, we'll ship him over to my Bronx headquarters, prepare him for experimentation."

"Again?" Tom yawned noisily. "Didn't your stooges find out enough the last time you had me tied up?"

"*This,*" Takapa snapped, "will be the last time."

"I know what you want," Tom informed him, trying to sound confident, hoping to catch them off balance. "You're after the same thing as Stacy— lupine DNA. Once you've got that isolated, you can *really* refine her serum—"

"And make my army the strongest, the most vicious it can be. Bravo," said Takapa dryly. "But it's more than that. With the 'wolf factor fully synthesized and in my control, I can create a lupine toxin that will overcome the defenses of even the strongest resister. Everyone we bite will turn, no exceptions."

Marcie nodded. "Think how many humans Takapa's army will be able to turn in a single night."

"And then what? You make sure they all take your serum and get full control of them?"

213

"It's all in the marketing," purred Takapa. "Those who embrace the 'wolf will be told it makes them faster, makes their senses keener. Those who try to reject the 'wolf, well—we'll just sell it to them as a cure."

Marcie smiled. "There will be other idiots like Stacy Stein, desperate to help these poor victims."

"So the world gets flooded with random 'wolves?" Tom looked at Marcie for confirmation, and she nodded. "Doesn't that go against all the old-fashioned stuff about quality and purity that 'wolves like you believe in?"

"These street trash 'wolves will be an inferior race. Servants to the true breed—and, through the drug, dependent on us." She smiled. "They will do anything for their pureblood masters."

"So that's what makes it acceptable to polite 'wolf society, huh? A whole new race of soldiers and servants." He repressed a shudder. "And you really think the rest of the world will just sit back and watch you create a werewolf nation?"

"We're not fools," said Takapa. "We're realists. We'll start small. I am furnishing the next generations of 'wolves with the tools and knowledge they'll need if they are to flourish. I am going to unite the 'wolves as never before." He punched his fist into his palm. "It will truly be *das Zeitalter des Werwolfs*."

"Wolf time," Tom translated. "With the support of a dried-up pureblood bitch and the stolen biology of resisters like me and Rico."

214

Marcie slapped him hard in the face.

Takapa leaned in close. His breath stank of raw meat. "Once I overcome that boy's resistance, there will be no human defense that can stand against me."

"Oh yeah? Not even Jicaque?"

Takapa reacted angrily. "That old crank is nothing. He's used up."

"So why do you flare up even at the sound of his name?" asked Tom before turning to Marcie. "And why did you frighten him out of New Orleans with death threats? Just for laughs?"

Takapa seemed to have stopped listening. "You are a wereling," he said in a distant tone, as if he were giving a lecture. "Your dual nature is near perfectly balanced; you draw on the best of your humanity and the best of the 'wolf. Once I crack the genetic code that allows you to do this, I can use it to enhance the natures of the most loyal soldiers. They'll mate with pureblood females and sire a new breed, more powerful and deadly than ever."

Tom looked away. "Spare me the global domination crap. You're crazy."

"No, he's not," said Marcie. "And Kate will help us in that task. She'll be a most fertile 'wolf mother over the coming years, however loudly she howls about it."

"You'll have to find her first," Tom taunted.

"I will," Marcie calmly assured him. "Let's go, Takapa. My husband has been out searching for

Kate, but he'll be joining us shortly. We should get ready for tonight. It's almost time."

Tom noticed a clock on the wall. It was eleven o'clock.

In an hour, the slaughter would begin.

Despite the fear, despite the tension, Kate found herself catnapping in her tiny prison. She felt totally exhausted, feverish almost. When Swagger opened up her locker and dragged her out onto the floor, she barely reacted.

"Time to get you ready for your big night," Swagger said. "Let's go."

Two familiar henchmen, Shaun and Eric, hauled her up without comment and pulled her out of the locker room.

"You know, your daddy's come to watch the show too," Swagger informed her. "Quite a reunion. Shame you'll miss out on it."

Kate felt doubly dismayed. To know her father was condoning this horror . . . Her mother had been psychotic most of her life; Kate expected nothing better of her—but her dad had always been cautious and careful. He hunted only sparingly and had always tried to keep Marcie's bloodlust under control.

Often he'd failed. Perhaps now he had given up entirely.

"I thought about leaving you in the locker till the fighting was over," Swagger told her lightly as they moved through the dingy corridors, "then giving you to the winners. Kind of a flesh trophy, you know?" He flashed that macabre smile at her. "But then I thought: Nah. I'm going to give you a real ringside seat."

Kate closed her eyes as fear crept back into her body. She didn't bother to ask his meaning. She knew she'd find out soon enough.

Swagger kicked open the double doors that led onto the rink; this must be the same route she'd seen Eric lead the fighters down when she was here before. A dark, brooding atmosphere hovered over the quiet arena, a cold air of anticipation.

Between two of the supporting pillars that ringed the arena, a length of chicken wire had been strung like a hammock about twenty feet above the floor.

"What's this?" she asked.

"Your hiding place, sweetheart," said Swagger. "See, that wire net there's going to hold the victory feast. Three hundred pounds of raw, tender meat—spiked with serum, of course—and little old you packed in alongside." He giggled like a kid. "When Takapa calls the winners, my boys slash those ropes and—*whoosh!*—down comes the food."

Kate shuddered. "And me with it." To be eaten alive.

"You got the idea." Swagger nodded.

"But Takapa needs me!" she argued desperately.

"You really should have been nice to me, sweetheart. I don't know what your mommy and the boss had planned for your pretty little ass, but they ain't going to get it now."

"They'll know you did this," she whispered. "They'll kill you."

"No, they won't. They'll just think you were hiding out here, trying to find a way to rescue your boyfriend Tom, and—oh, dear . . ."

Kate tried to rise, but her legs were too cramped. "Tom's here?"

"I heard he really misses you." Swagger wiped a make-believe tear from one of his eyes. "He's all torn up over it. Well—he will be."

Swagger guffawed with laughter and looked at Shaun and Eric. They managed a couple of sycophantic snickers but turned at the sound of an electric engine getting closer. Some kind of forklift truck was coming slowly across the stained concrete, piled high with boxes.

"Meat wagon," Swagger announced with evident pleasure. "We're ready to roll. Tie her up, gag her, then let's get her up there."

Kate recoiled, but she knew she had nowhere to run.

Tom struggled against the ropes that bound him until his wrists were raw. The situation seemed hopeless as the hands on the clock edged closer to midnight. He pictured Takapa and Marcie and Hal, her husband, talking and sipping cocktails upstairs together like VIPs, looking forward to their midnight arrival as guests of honor for the big fight.

A sound from outside startled him—a loud thump against the wall, then a dragging, sliding sort of noise.

The door handle turned. Someone was coming to get him. Tom braced himself.

Polar stood in the doorway, the hood of his gray sweatshirt hiding his face as ever, hands thrust in his pockets. Slowly he advanced.

Tom strained against his bonds, but it was useless.

Then Polar crouched down in front of him. "I told you not to miss—what the hell happened back there?" he said.

It was Jasmine's voice.

She shrugged off the hood. "Well, dumbass?"

Tom slumped back with relief. "A guy came in through the window. Hit me from behind."

"Typical," muttered Jasmine, roughly untying his knots.

He flinched as the ropes chafed against his raw skin. "So, you and Polar swapped outfits or something?"

"Polar won't be wearing anything but a body bag," she said brusquely. Now that Tom looked more closely, he could see dark stains stiffening the sweatshirt's material. "We broke in through the locker room. Place was empty; Polar was just lying there, beaten up bad. Stacy said she don't give much for his chances."

"Stacy's here?"

"We're all here, Tommy."

"Kate too?"

"Ain't seen her. But your Indian pal with the weird name is here."

He blinked in disbelief. "Jicaque?"

"Uh-huh. Regular rescue squad." She regarded him sternly. "Do you think I'd walk out on you just 'cause you're a dumb jerk with no taste?"

He smiled to himself. "Not for a second."

"Good. Else you'd be a dumb jerk with no balls, too."

The ropes came free, and Tom gratefully massaged his tender wrists. "Jicaque's here to stop the fight?"

Jasmine shrugged. "Sure hope he's got something planned. Him and the others are waiting in the lobby, out of sight. I came here alone—no one noticed me dressed like this." They crossed to the door and she indicated the unconscious thug who'd been guarding his door. "Not till it was too late, anyway. Come on."

As they sprinted down the corridor, Tom heard a plaintive *beep-beep* sound from Jasmine's wrist-watch.

"Midnight," she breathed.

Kate was half buried beneath a pile of raw meat. It was hard to breathe, but maybe that was a blessing since the stench was so disgusting. The feel of the cold, dead flesh on her skin was almost unbearable. Her clothes were saturated with rancid blood, and the weight of it all was crushing her.

And now the gladiators were entering the arena, herded in by a handful of Swagger's goons armed with automatic weapons. The prisoners shambled in, two hundred or more, ranging from kids no older than Rico to bag lady types in their fifties.

Kate stared in horror as the people split off into groups and took up positions around the rink, some directly beneath her, facing each other in groups of twenty or so. They were silent, their faces blank, their sunken eyes dark and burning. The armed guards ranged themselves around the rink. A spiteful charge was building in the air.

"Listen up, everyone." Swagger's voice reverberated around the arena. "Before we begin . . . a few words from our leader: Papa Takapa."

There was no applause, no real reaction at all. A few of the fighters turned to gaze upon the man they were fighting for, the scrawny albino who stood in the front row of the bleachers beside Swagger. A few rows back Kate saw her parents. She squirmed, tried to rock the hammock, to get herself noticed; she would do anything to delay the proceedings. But she could barely move beneath the mass of raw meat.

"Greetings, my warriors," Takapa said. *Oh, what a pompous ass,* Kate thought. "You stand before me now because you have survived a number of trials by combat. Those who fight and triumph tonight shall rank as officers in my private army. You shall enjoy power and privilege, a place in the new order I am bringing to the lupine community." He paused impressively. "In ancient Rome there were many kinds of gladiator. The Samnite, a helmeted warrior with sword and armor . . . the Thracian, with his curved dagger and shield of bronze . . . Retarius, the net fighter, a bloodied trident clamped in his hand . . ."

Kate surveyed the motley crowd shifting impatiently about below her, muttering and whispering. They seemed unimpressed with Takapa's lecture. Perhaps he guessed this, because he cut it short.

"But you! You are a fresh breed of gladiator, a new invention. You have no weapons save your cunning and your savagery. No armor save the toughened hide of the magnificent creatures you can become. Fight well for me in your factions, and you shall no longer be caged. I shall bestow honor on you, give you purpose. You will be allowed to serve me and all our kind."

Again he paused, and this time the people in the arena stayed silent.

"I promise you blood!" he shouted, exultant. "I promise you carnage. I promise you the future. Now—*fight!*"

No one moved. One or two of the guards raised

their weapons threateningly.

Had the emperor Nero ever had this kind of trouble? Kate thought darkly.

Then Swagger rose to his feet. "You want your next fix? Get going! Now!"

That got to them. A few halfhearted scuffles broke out amid the different factions. Soon the skirmishes were escalating to full-on fistfights—and suddenly everyone was getting caught up in the fighting. Throughout the arena men and women were shouting, threatening, throttling, tearing into each other just like she'd witnessed before but on a much grander scale.

Suddenly the wire mesh hammock supporting her lurched. She felt herself drop a fraction. One of the ropes lashed around the concrete pillars, securing the vast net in place, was giving way under the sheer weight of the doctored meat. It slipped again. The net tilted a little to the left, then a little more, threatening to ditch its haul.

If the hammock gave way, she would plunge down into the heart of the bloody battle.

CHAPTER SEVENTEEN

Tom followed Jasmine down into the arena's dirty lobby. Stacy and Rico came out from behind a crumbling concrete pillar as they arrived. "Are my parents safe?" he asked Stacy.

She nodded. "And looking pretty perky, considering the number of scary viruses they're carrying." She fanned her face with her hand. "It was kind of hairy for a while, but the plan worked."

"When you didn't come out of the hotel, we knew the 'wolves snatched you, so we went back to Park East," Rico said, chewing noisily on some gum. "There were all these weird guys there in, like, radiation suits or something."

"Hazard squad," Stacy explained. "Your parents are isolated. No one can get to them."

"Shame we can't say the same about us," said Jasmine, looking around nervously.

"And while I was busy organizing everything for them," Stacy went on, "some thugs ransacked my laboratory. Took all the serum samples I had."

"I heard Takapa discuss it with Swagger," Tom said. "He and Marcie will be in the arena now. The fighting must have started. I *wish* I knew where Kate was."

Stacy looked surprised. "I thought she'd be locked up with you."

"Takapa and Marcie said they were still looking for her. So either she escaped from Swagger or else . . ." Tom sighed. "Where's Jicaque? How'd you hook up with him?"

Stacy frowned as she stared about into the shadows that pooled thickly in each corner of the lobby. "He was waiting in my lab at the hospital—he came and found me, said he was here to gather us; that we would be allies for one final battle. But now I don't know—"

"I'm here."

Tom whirled around to find Jicaque standing suddenly right behind him, wearing a long dark overcoat over a shabby linen suit. His deep brown eyes seemed troubled. "Tell me, Tom, have the poor souls caged in the locker room been given their fix of Stacy's serum?"

"I guess so," Tom reported. "They were due a dose at six."

Jicaque nodded gravely. "There'll be terrible bloodshed tonight."

"So what do we do?" Jasmine wondered aloud. "I guess getting the hell out of here ain't an option?"

"Not without Kate," Tom said.

Jicaque nodded. "We've got to get inside the arena. Stop this madness once and for all."

"Nice thought," said Stacy. "Any practical ideas how we do that?"

But Jicaque had already turned on his heel and was striding away, his long silver hair trailing behind him like a comet's tail, his dark overcoat flapping about his ankles.

He led them along a dank corridor and up a flight of crumbling stairs. "This leads to the upper tiers of the seating," Jicaque informed them. "The lower entrances are blocked to prevent any escape attempts."

The stairway ended in a set of peeling double doors. Beyond them, rising in volume, the unmistakable sounds of violent battle carried: shouts and crashes and shrieks of agony.

Jicaque tried the doors, but they wouldn't budge. Tom lent his weight, pulling on the handles with all his strength, but it was a hopeless task. The doors were locked.

"They don't want no one getting in, neither," Rico observed, wheezing a little after climbing so many stairs.

"You taken your inhaler?" Jasmine prompted him.

Rico pulled the puffer moodily from his pocket. "I keep saying, it don't work."

"Let me see it," Jicaque snapped.

Rico produced the inhaler and Jicaque extracted the little pressurized canister from the plastic housing. "Yes," he muttered, "that might just do." He delved in his pocket and pulled out a few crumbs and lumps of some silvery white powder.

Stacy watched him. "What's that?"

"Jicaque?" Tom looked at him uncertainly. "Is that more of your magnesium?"

"Rubber band," Jicaque snapped, holding out his other hand.

Jasmine obliged him with a band from her hair, giving Tom a puzzled glance. "Magnesium?"

Tom nodded. "He powders the ends of cigarettes with the stuff. If he's in trouble, he lights up and the magnesium blinds whoever's close by."

"Cool," said Rico happily.

Jicaque secured the white lumps to the canister with the rubber band. "Now, Rico, that gum you're chewing."

Rico handed over the gum, and Jicaque used it to fix the little canister to the lock on the door. But as he produced a disposable lighter from his pocket, Stacy snatched it away.

"You can't set fire to that stuff!" Stacy said, appalled. "That's a pressurized container."

Jicaque shrugged, untied a string from one of his scruffy silver braids of hair. "And *that* is a locked door. Any other suggestions?"

Suddenly the lighter was out of Stacy's hand and back in Jicaque's. He struck the flint and a flame jumped from its end. "Tell me, Tom, have you heard of Chet Baker? Great jazz musician."

Tom shook his head wearily. "Is this the time for a history lesson?"

Jicaque shook his head disapprovingly. "You haven't heard a trumpet till you hear Chet speak through it." He paused, apparently transfixed by the smoky flame. "You know, jazz is a lot like life. All a matter of timing." He set the flame to the string, his makeshift fuse. "Back down the stairs, everyone."

Tom covered his eyes as the magnesium compound flared with blinding intensity. Jicaque shooed him away down to the turn in the stairwell to join the others.

With a deafening blast the canister exploded.

"So much for Rico's inhaler." Stacy sighed.

"Guess it *does* work," Rico said, a slow grin spreading over his face.

Tom peered around the corner. The door was blackened; the lock had been punched right out.

"Now the danger begins," Jicaque murmured. "Who's with me?"

"I am." Tom glanced around at Jasmine, Stacy, and Rico. "But maybe you guys should hang back here and—"

"Forget it," said Jasmine.

"People might get hurt," said Stacy. "I can help."

And Rico nodded too. "Time to get even."

"Then let's go," the old man said, moving off into the wreaths of smoke coiling from the charred hole in the door.

Kate had finally managed to work her mouth free of the tape that gagged her. She bit and chewed at the knotted ropes that bound her wrists. All around the arena the fighting was escalating, far more savage than the scrappy bouts she'd witnessed before. Swagger was right: These people had been trained, conditioned to fight for their survival.

Across the arena in the bleachers she saw her mother watching rapt beside Takapa. Her father looked on at the spectacle impassively. If she could only signal to him . . .

She gasped as the net lurched and dropped another few inches. Giant chunks of meat went tumbling as the net tilted and fell around the maniacs fighting below.

A woman looked up wildly, as if suspecting an attack from above. It was the bleached blonde who'd tricked Polar back in the locker room. Her eyes were gleaming yellow. Saliva flooded from her jaws as her body began to warp into lupine form.

Kate knew what a tempting target she must make, trapped here helpless, surrounded by a half ton of bloody flesh, and she knew with horrid certainty the woman meant to kill her. Sure enough, with a frenzied roar the blonde leapt for the net, her broken nails extending into talons mid-jump.

The creature scraped against the chicken wire close to Kate's head, then fell back down. Kate realized she was still out of reach. But for how much longer?

A man rushed to tackle the blonde before her metamorphosis was complete, pounding his fists down on her distorted face. But others had noticed that the net was disgorging its bloody haul. And more of the fighters were starting to turn.

Kate tugged at her bonds with a new desperation. The net shook again and she saw that another 'wolf had jumped up and was hanging from the thick chicken wire by its claws. But the metal soon gave way and the animal fell with a thud.

Then suddenly Kate heard a sharp, percussive crack. Before the echoes had died away, the entire arena seemed to shake with a single bellowed cry.

"Enough."

The sound lashed around the arena like a steely whip.

The 'wolves slowed in their struggles, then stopped altogether, panting hard, backing off from their private fights and scenting the air for this noisy interloper.

Swagger's guards patrolling the perimeter raised their weapons, searching for the intruder through rifle sights.

Kate saw Tom standing at the top of the steps

that led down through the bleachers, Jasmine, Rico, and Stacy standing alongside him. In front of Tom was a slight, elderly, silver-maned man. All eyes, human and beast, were on him now.

"Please," Kate muttered, shutting her eyes. "Please, Jicaque, make this good."

Tom stared as the 'wolves in the arena paused in a sudden, uneasy truce, as if acting on some deeper instinct.

He felt sick with fear. There were so many of the creatures in here, trampling human corpses beneath their paws as they milled around the blood-soaked rink. At any moment the violence might ignite again—and all that was stopping the 'wolves from taking the fight out of the arena and into the bleachers were a few of Swagger's generals with guns. Guns that were aimed now at him and Jicaque, guns that would tear them apart in a single burst of fire.

Hal and Marcie Folan rose from their seats. Hal looked at Tom without emotion, but Marcie's lip kept twitching as she watched him, like she was about to bare her teeth. She kept glancing at Takapa impatiently; this was his territory, Tom supposed, and she was giving him a chance to handle the situation. How long before her patience was spent?

Takapa too had risen, his face contorting into odd expressions as he struggled to find an appropriate way to express his rage. He turned to Swagger.

"Get down there," he said in a low voice, gesturing to the rink. "Make sure the scum don't get out of hand. This won't take long."

Swagger hesitated, glaring at Tom hungrily. Then he turned and started down the steps as ordered.

Takapa's pink eyes blazed furiously at Jicaque. "You dare to interfere?" he said hoarsely at last. *"Now?"*

"I let you alone for too long," Jicaque said calmly. "That was my mistake."

"No. Coming here tonight was your mistake," Takapa snarled. He looked past Jicaque to face Stacy. "The rumors of your death are exaggerated, I see."

"Don't look at me—I didn't start them," said Stacy.

Takapa smiled, then gestured to the bloody rink, to the beasts that prowled there. "But you started all this."

"And I'll help finish it," she said fiercely.

Tom felt someone tug on his arm. Rico. He was pointing across the vast arena. Tom cursed. Unseen by Takapa, Marcie, and the rest, someone was balanced up on a mountain of meat hanging above the rink, waving furiously. "Kate," he breathed.

"I'll sneak down, help her out," Rico whispered.

"Stay out of it, Rico," Tom warned him. "You're only a kid; you can't—"

"Watch me." With that, Rico slipped into the bleachers to Tom's right.

Tom held his breath, but miraculously, it seemed no one had seen him go.

Then Jicaque spoke, and Tom's attention snapped back to the bleachers.

"I suppose," said Jicaque thoughtfully, "that Dr. Stein could be said to be the founder of the feast here." His voice hardened. "Shame the feast is poisoned."

Takapa narrowed his pink eyes. "What nonsense is this?"

"The drug you've been synthesizing, the means of controlling your rabid army here . . ." Jicaque waved a hand at the teeming monsters in the rink. "Your people stole the doctored samples from Stacy's laboratory, and I guessed you would be using them tonight. So before the supplies were taken, I did some herbal doctoring of my own."

"Well, whatever you did, you wasted your time," snarled Takapa. "The contents of those test tubes were added to my own stocks of the drug."

Tom held his breath. But Jicaque just smiled. "Well, then, I contaminated your entire supply."

Takapa was shaking his head now in angry disbelief. "No. You're lying," he snapped. "Are you blind? They *are* fighting for me!"

"As humans, sure." Jicaque clicked his fingers. "But now that they've transformed to the lupine state, my herbs are taking effect."

Tom gripped Jicaque's arm. "The cure? It's working on them now?"

"The first step of many—the restoration of human will. But I can only cure those who want to be cured," Jicaque reminded him in a low voice. "There are many here who like the power their 'wolf lends them."

"It's a trick!" Takapa spat with the fury of a cheated child. "A filthy trick!"

"For your sake, Takapa," said Marcie, "it had better be."

The albino raised his arms and fell forward into a crouching position. His form seemed to blur and run like watercolors in the rain.

Tom flinched as a lean, sinewy 'wolf suddenly faced them, eyes narrowed and burning with malice.

"Another mistake," Jicaque announced calmly. "As a 'wolf you can't issue orders to your men." The old man raised his voice, cupped his hands to his mouth. "Listen! Takapa tried to use you, to make you fight for his own ends. But now you're free from the hold he has over you!"

With a roar of hatred the rangy white 'wolf arched its back and then pounced forward, jaws snapping for the old man's throat.

CHAPTER EIGHTEEN

Tom shoved Jicaque out of the way. The old man staggered and fell between two benches.

Jasmine shrieked as Takapa landed at her feet. She kicked him hard in the head with her pointed boots. The werewolf growled, swiped at her with one massive paw, but Jasmine leapt for cover among the rotting wooden benches. Enraged, the creature moved to follow.

"Rise up!" Jicaque shouted at the 'wolves pacing the arena. "Fight for yourselves now, against the people who've used you!"

"All right, enough!" Marcie bawled. "Swagger, kill him!"

Swagger didn't need telling twice. He opened fire, spraying the gangway with bullets. One by one his generals joined in the attack. Stacy dived for cover back through the double doors, and Jicaque huddled down behind the benches in front.

Takapa broke off his attack on Jasmine, staring around in confusion. Bullets whistled through the cold air. But then the white 'wolf saw Jicaque in his hiding place and readied himself to pounce once again.

"No!" Tom shouted, and threw himself at the creature, locking his arm around its sinewy throat. Takapa bucked and writhed, snapped at him, but Tom was just out of range of the monster's dagger-like teeth and holding on for dear life. Finally Takapa threw himself into a full body roll. Tom couldn't hold on, and his bad shoulder smashed against the concrete of the gangway. He cried out in pain—then he heard a howl of anger. Dazed, he opened his eyes.

Jicaque was nowhere to be seen.

But the low growl, the bestial eyes narrowed in his direction, told Tom that Takapa had found a new target. He tried to pull himself away, but the 'wolf was preparing to spring.

"Get out of here, you fool!"

Takapa reacted to the voice as if stung.

Marcie was shouting at him. "Come on! We can't fight them all!"

Takapa turned in confusion.

"My God," breathed Tom.

A whole pack of werewolves had broken free of the confines of the rink. Swagger was no longer firing at Tom and his friends but into the slavering mass of enraged werewolves. The creatures were thinking for themselves now, acting on their own unfettered instincts.

And clearly they wanted revenge.

Marcie and Hal were running for an emergency exit to their left, pursued by eight or nine of the lupine monsters. They dropped down to the ground and brought on the change as they fled.

Takapa roared in defiance at Tom one final time, then chased after them, hurdling the benches in the bleachers, a white blur disappearing into the shadows.

Tom nodded grimly as Hal and Marcie smashed through the emergency exit and vanished from view, Takapa close on their heels. But the rattle of more gunfire riveted Tom's attention back to events in the arena. The men were firing wildly; some of the beasts bayed in pain as the bullets tore into them. But there was no way Swagger and his generals could take them all. The 'wolves had been trained well and now were using their skills to slash their persecutors to ribbons.

Tom swallowed hard as he looked at Kate, still perched high on her mountain of carcasses. She waved with both arms, trying to be sure he'd seen her, and Tom waved back. But his stomach was churning. How could he get to her, caught between bullets and claws—and where was Rico?

Turning, he staggered over to Jasmine, who was shakily getting to her feet. "You okay?"

"Sure," she gasped. "I'm good."

Stacy sat up from a row of bleachers, rubbing her head and wincing. "What happened to Jicaque?

Is he . . . ?" Her hand flew to her mouth. "Jesus. How long was I out?"

It was true. In seconds everything had turned around. Now, with Takapa and his guests gone, scores of 'wolves were roaming the bleachers, howling. Many more were feeding on the corpses of their fallen opponents—and the men with guns who had sought to control them. Swagger himself was nowhere to be seen, but two of his surviving generals were standing back to back beside one of the supporting pillars, terror in their eyes, shooting at any lupine who came too near.

I can only cure those who want to be cured, Jicaque had said, and clearly some of the 'wolves craved more violence, more blood; a few ringleaders were snapping at their fellows, trying to pick up the fight like nothing had happened.

"Some of the 'wolves are changing back," Stacy realized. "They'll become targets for the others, just like we are." She set off through the tiers of seating, heading for a young girl who stood naked and shivering, gazing around the arena in shock. "We have to help them."

"Maybe round them up into a group," Tom called, and Stacy nodded distractedly.

And then Tom saw it. The net supporting Kate had started to give way; it was sagging seriously at one end. Huge hunks of meat were tumbling into the arena, exciting the waiting 'wolves that paced below. But seeing their hungry eyes, Tom knew they craved soft, tender, wholly human flesh.

Jasmine looked around, suddenly panicked. "Where's Rico?"

"Trying to reach Kate," Tom said worriedly. "I couldn't stop him."

Jasmine looked appalled. "He'll get himself killed!"

"Work your way around the stands," Tom told her, signaling the direction Rico had taken. "I'll take the direct route." He ran down the gangway, mercifully free of wandering 'wolves, picking up speed as he hurtled down the steps. He had to reach her, save her somehow before—

"Hey, freak," shouted Swagger, jumping up from his hiding place near the front of the bleachers. He wielded his gun like a club and brought it around in a savage arc.

Tom couldn't stop in time. The weapon caught him under the chin and he fell reeling back.

Swagger advanced on him, gun raised. "Guess who?"

"The tooth fairy?" Tom spat out a thick gobbet of blood. "Say, Swagger, are you out of bullets, or did you just forget how your gun works?"

"Don't need bullets for you."

Tom heard a whistling rattle as the wire netting holding Kate was attacked by another 'wolf. He knew he couldn't waste any time. "It's over,

Swagger," he yelled. "Now get out of my way."

"You ruined everything!" Swagger bellowed, his scarred face livid red, eyes screwed up in rage. "I was going to *be* somebody. I was going to count!"

"I don't have time for this!" Tom hurled himself at Swagger, hoping to knock him over, but there was true madness in the thug's eyes now. His big hand closed around Tom's throat and threw him flat on his back on the concrete.

"What's wrong with you? You fought good last night. You really hurt me, man."

Tom heard Kate yell in alarm. He tried to get up, but Swagger pushed him back down to the ground.

"Now you're going to hurt too." Swagger's crazed eyes shone with malice. "And so's your girlfriend."

"No!" Tom heard the guttural edge to his own voice, heard Kate scream again for help, felt the anger flooding through him. Swagger was laughing at him, his eyes burning yellow, his features beginning to bulge and twist into bestial form.

"You took away everything I had that was good," the big man said. "Nothing left but the bad now." He crouched down in front of Tom. "Want to see?"

He was starting to shake. Thick, coarse blond hair was curling from his hands and face. His jaw extended outward, his teeth began to jut out sharply from his red gums.

But the change was on Tom too. As his fear, his anger, all those dark emotions pounded through his body and urged on the metamorphosis, he knew that this fight wouldn't be over until one of them was dead.

Now that she'd untied herself, ready for escape, Kate found she had precisely nowhere to go. She was clinging onto the remnants of the chicken wire hammock for dear life; it was hanging down almost vertically from the pillar. Many of the 'wolves, their anger spent and Takapa's hold on them broken, had ceased fighting; they were roaming about the stands, transforming back one by one into their human forms. Stacy was going to them each in turn, trying to give help and comfort.

The firing had all stopped now, the last of Swagger's henchmen split open by razor claws the second he'd run out of ammo. But there was still danger in the arena.

Like the two lupines prowling around below her.

One was gray and wasted, the other bloated and black. The creatures were surprisingly single-minded amid the chaos in the rink; the stretch of wire just beyond her toes had been ripped clear away by their teeth and claws, and she doubted they were about to give up now.

Her fingers were red, the mesh biting into them so keenly she'd lost all sensation. She sensed the beasts beneath her willing her to give up, to slip and fall right into their drooling jaws.

Kate looked away, trying to blank them out, and saw Tom running toward her. She cried out in dismay as Swagger burst out and ambushed him.

Now Swagger was turning 'wolf, and so was Tom. Clothes split and fell away, bones bent and cracked as the metamorphosis ran its course. Finally she was watching two animals warily circle each other on all fours, Tom sleek and well proportioned, Swagger the biggest, mangiest 'wolf in the arena.

Tom's eyes had remained brown; he was his old self, the savagery of Stacy's drug out of his system. But the knowledge sent a spasm of fear through Kate. Against the lupine Swagger, wereling Tom with his human scruples didn't stand a chance.

She gasped as the gray 'wolf leaped up at her again. This time its jaws snagged one of her sneakers, wrenched it from her left foot. "Get away from me!" she yelled.

Right. Like it would listen.

But someone had heard her.

"Hey, Kate!"

The hoarse whisper barely carried over the snarling of the two 'wolves, but Kate recognized the voice at once. "Rico? Where are you?"

A small olive-skinned face emerged over the rink's crash barrier. "Listen up. I'll lead those two away; you drop down and run like hell. Is it a deal?"

"Rico, get out of here!" she hissed. "Get help!"

She saw that Tom had tried to dodge past

Swagger to reach the rink. But Swagger had moved with incredible speed, swiping Tom's hind legs from under him. He somersaulted through the air and splashed down hard in a puddle of blood.

"No!" she yelled. And her fingers were slipping. Below her the 'wolves were licking their bloody chops in anticipation.

"Hey, boys," a supercilious voice called. "Either of you two got a light?"

Kate turned her head to find Jasmine leaning casually against the crash barrier, with three cigarettes in her lips. Rico was peeping out from behind her.

The gray 'wolf emitted a low roar at the sight of these new prospective morsels, and its partner's drool hung from its jaws in great sticky strings. They approached Jasmine cautiously, as if suspecting a trap. But she was just standing there.

The beasts drew closer, *closer.*

Rico passed her a lighter. "Sorry, boys," she said coldly, "I found one already." She closed her eyes and placed the flame to the tips of the cigarettes—which flared like blowtorches.

The gray, skinny wolf gave a shrill, ululating howl and skittered away. But the dark one was enraged. It lunged forward, jaws opened wide to take off her head.

Jasmine dodged, took one of the burning cigarettes, and stubbed it out on the creature's snout.

243

Flames licked at its muzzle. It roared in terrible pain and bounded away. "I'm not running anymore!" she screamed after it. "You hear me?"

Kate dropped down to the filthy concrete, half blinded, her stinging fingers red-hot and numb. She tried desperately to blink away the bright blobs on her vision left by the light show. "What the hell brand are those?" she gasped.

"Jicaque's special smokes," she heard Jasmine mutter.

As her vision started to clear, Kate saw that Swagger had batted Tom back to the ground. He looked a gory mess, his coat matted black with blood—how much was his and how much he'd rolled in, she couldn't tell. Before he could get to his feet, the Swagger 'wolf was on top of him, stamping down on his rib cage. His sharp teeth raked a crimson line along Tom's throat.

Rico broke free of Jasmine's grip and raced across the rink to where the two 'wolves struggled.

"No!" Jasmine yelled. "*Parate*, Rico! There's nothing you can do!"

Then everything seemed to be happening in slow motion.

Rico was sprinting across the bloody arena, his breath coming in short puffs, steaming into the icy air.

Kate and Jasmine were running after him.

Too slow.

As Swagger opened his massive jaws to scissor

through Tom's neck, Rico shoulder-charged him. Swagger growled and snapped instinctively at Rico's arm, his teeth sinking into the boy's flesh. The sharp yellow teeth were soon bright red with blood. Rico screamed with pain—but Swagger howled louder.

The huge 'wolf twisted and writhed, his jaws foaming, his deep, bellowing roars modulating to high-pitched screams as he switched back to his human form in a series of sick spasms. It was like he'd swallowed acid and now it was burning its way through his entire body.

Finally he lay still, eyes dull and glazed, a thick white froth seeping from his cracked mouth.

As she ran to reach Tom and Rico, it dawned on Kate what she had just witnessed. Rico was a total resister—the boy's blood was deadly poison to the 'wolves. That was why Stacy and Takapa had both treasured it so in their research.

Swagger the man might have known that—but Swagger the 'wolf had seen just another piece of meat. All sense blinded by bloodlust, he'd become the final victim of his own violence.

But Kate's eyes filled with tears as she covered the final distance. Who had he taken with him?

CHAPTER NINETEEN

Jasmine reached Rico a second before Kate did. She scooped him up from where he lay slumped against Tom's prone body. Rico's eyes were rolling back in his head; his arm was a mauled mess. That treasured blood was everywhere, spurting out in quick pulses from his torn flesh.

"Stacy!" Kate yelled, panting for breath. "We need you! Quick!" Her voice echoed.

An eerie calm was settling over the arena. The surviving 'wolves had either slunk away to freedom or else changed back to human form, huddling together in small groups among the corpses. Stacy was hurrying toward them—how much time did they have?

"Shit, Rico," Jasmine muttered through her tears. "Don't you dare leave me alone. You hear me?"

Rico coughed, his eyelids fluttering like he was falling asleep. *"Mucha sangre?"*

"Only a little," she whispered soothingly. "It's only bleeding a little."

Rico closed his eyes. "Sure . . . Thanks, Jas."

Kate turned to Tom. She heard his back twist and crack as his body straightened, his rib cage snap and flutter as it shrank in on itself; watched his regular human features return. She found a shawl and draped it around him like a blanket.

"Sorry," he croaked, dabbing at the sticky gash on his neck. "I couldn't reach you. I was useless."

Kate squeezed his hand. "No, you weren't," she said, remembering the savagery that had possessed him on the bridge. "You were *you.*"

Tom scrambled up, and went to help Jasmine. "Rico?" White-faced and scared, he looked down at the boy. "You saved my life."

"We quits now, yeah?" Rico's eyes were unfocused. "Swagger dead?"

Tom glanced over and nodded grimly. "Very."

"Good," muttered Rico. He was starting to shake. "Jas? You think Ramon'd be proud of me? Like, real proud?"

She nodded, tears falling down her face. "Real proud, Rico."

Rico smiled. "It'll be good to see my bro again."

"You're not seeing him yet," Stacy snapped. "Look at my fingers instead. How many do you see?"

"Want to go sleep," Rico mumbled.

"Look! How many do you see?" Stacy insisted.

"I dunno." Rico raised his good arm feebly and gave her the finger. "How many do *you* see?"

Stacy grinned. "That's it. Stay with me, Rico. Give up now and Ramon's going to kick your ass."

"Screw you. Want to sleep now."

"I mean it. Stay with me!" Stacy laid Rico down on the grimy floor and studied his grisly arm, hard faced and professional. "We have to find the brachial artery and close it off," she said. "Keep him from losing any more blood. We need a tourniquet."

"Look out!" Tom yelled, looking over her shoulder.

A 'wolf was dragging itself along the concrete toward them. Kate backed away, looking for a weapon. But the monster looked weak. In its jaws it held something.

A Polaroid camera.

"The camera strap," Stacy ordered. "Get it."

Kate cautiously pulled the camera free of the creature's jaws. It growled and watched her closely. She removed the strap and gave it to Stacy, who tied it around Rico's arm. The 'wolf quieted down when Kate placed the camera back in front of it.

A minute later it was Polar lying there, curled up in a ball, his body covered in bruises. He was sobbing quietly, clutching the camera.

"Must've found the locker key after all," murmured Kate.

Jasmine looked at him coldly. "Kind of late to help us now," she said. "Him and that damn camera."

"Guess we all need to cling to something," Tom said quietly.

Kate shivered, felt a presence behind her. She turned to find Jicaque hovering a few yards away.

"Where did you go?" Tom demanded.

"Called an ambulance," said Jicaque. "The way to the locker rooms is clear. Paramedics are on their way. Bring Rico there to be taken to the hospital." He looked at Stacy intently. "Tell the paramedics Rico was attacked by a wild dog." He glanced around and sighed. "What really happened here must remain our secret. Think of the panic it could cause."

"But what about all these people?" Kate gestured to the groups huddled in the bleachers.

Jicaque shrugged. "I can help them. If they allow me to give them my treatment each day for a lunar month—"

"What about Polar?" Jasmine interrupted, nudging the curled-up figure at her feet with her boot. "You going to help him too?"

"Yes. But for now he should go with Rico. He'll recover." The old man looked at her meaningfully. "With help from his friends."

"Polar got no friends," said Jasmine, turning away. "Not anymore." She gently lifted Rico in both arms and carried him toward the locker rooms.

Stacy gently helped the weeping Polar to his feet and led him away. "We'll see you later," she called.

Tom raised a hand in farewell. Kate found she was shivering and hugged herself for warmth. "So. What happens now?"

"Takapa's notes," Tom said. "The results of his research. We should destroy them."

"Already done," Jicaque replied. "I wasn't just kicking back while you fought, you know." He smiled wanly. "We set back Takapa's plans tonight. But he won't give up. There is some greater purpose that consumes him. We need to find out what that is."

"We?" Kate raised an eyebrow. "Jicaque, Tom needs to be cured. He wants his life back. This isn't his fight." She looked at Tom. "Go on, tell him," she urged.

But Tom said nothing.

Jicaque smiled at Kate sadly. "I can only cure those who wish to be cured," he said softly.

"So?" Kate responded. *What's going on here?*

"Tom still has work to do. He does not wish to be cured. Not yet."

Kate stared at Tom. "He's wrong. Tell him he's wrong."

"I . . ." Tom took his hands away from Jicaque's and placed his palms on Kate's shoulders. "I can't." He looked into her eyes. "This thing isn't over yet. We'll never be free until it is."

"But this could be your only chance," she insisted. "You want to throw that away? You want to throw your whole *life* away?"

He shook his head. "There's more than just my life at stake, though, isn't there?" She said nothing. "You *know* there is."

"This isn't about me; don't bring me into this!"

Kate yelled, gesturing at the welt on his neck and the bruise on his chin. "I won't be responsible for your death too! Look at you! You were nearly killed tonight. And so many people have died. . . ."

"I wish I could just walk away." He shook his head. "I can't."

"Wait." She stared at him. "You enjoy it now, don't you? Lupine power. You *like* it."

"It's not that!" Tom grated. "How can you even *think* that?"

Kate turned away. "You don't know what I think, Tom."

"While I'm 'wolf, I can protect us till we're both out of this mess for good. Together!"

She wanted to shout at him: *If you weren't 'wolf, maybe we could* really *be together. Maybe we would stand a chance.*

But how could she now?

Without looking back, she set off for the locker rooms. She'd forgotten she only had one sneaker. It was hard to keep your dignity when you were walking lopsided.

"I should go after her," she heard Tom say.

"Maybe she needs a little space right now, huh?" the old man said.

I don't, Kate thought desperately. *I want you here with me, Tom. Come after me. Stop me.*

But her own uneven footsteps were the only ones echoing around the freezing arena.

CHAPTER TWENTY

That night Tom's thoughts were heavy with what Kate had said. He knew she was upset, she'd been through a hell of a lot. But he knew too that Jicaque was right. Takapa had to be stopped, whatever the risks—or none of them could ever rest easy again. If Tom could make more of a difference as a 'wolf, then he'd have to stay that way until this thing was over.

He caught up with Kate the next morning at Park East Hospital, feeling nervous as hell. She was lying on her side on the couch in Stacy's office, cleaned up from her ordeal and dressed in gray hospital pajamas like an inpatient. She looked like she'd been up all night, crying.

His heart sank like a stone. "Rico?"

"He's okay," she said, not meeting his gaze. "He lost a lot of blood, but he'll pull through."

"Thank God."

"Polar's stable too."

Tom nodded, standing awkwardly beside the door, uncertain what to say. "Have you been here all night?"

She nodded. "The ambulance was still there when I got outside. Stacy vouched for me, and they gave me a ride here."

"Would've been a long walk otherwise. Especially with one sneaker."

She didn't smile, but at least she looked directly at him. "How about you? Where've you been?"

"The arena. Jicaque was fixing people up."

"With deranged tailors?"

Tom glanced down at his ill-fitting jeans and shirt. "There was a whole load of old clothes down there. I guess for re-clothing the troops once they—" He broke off. "Anyway. I just wanted to watch him perform the first rituals of the cure."

It had been fascinating, watching the old man chant over the prone people, pressing his old, gnarled fingers against the pressure points of their bodies, warming the freezing air with the colorful words of his incantations.

She must have seen the faraway look on his face. "I'm sure it was something. Maybe he should charge admission."

Tom ignored her. It was what she did: coped with the world by holding it at arm's length.

"I tried calling you. . . ."

"I was asleep. Dead to the world." She half smiled. "Lucky for you, you didn't wake me. I feel a lot friendlier after a good long sleep."

Tom nodded. "I'm dying for a soft bed."

"Well, if you stay up all night . . . What about all the other walking wounded?"

"At another hospital, I think. Jicaque took care of it. . . . He's started work on the cure with them all."

She nodded. "Happy ending, then. Right?"

"I hope so."

They looked at each other for long, silent seconds.

Then Kate took a deep breath. "I was wrong to say what I did last night. . . ."

"You were upset. We were all upset." He cleared his throat. "I'm sorry I didn't go after you. I felt bad all night."

"Really?" she murmured. Her voice sounded hard, tired. "Well, I guess it's your issue. You've got to get through it your own way. Right?"

"Uh-huh." He paused. "You heard Jicaque: His cure takes a month. And I don't think we *have* a month before Takapa or your mom and dad try to catch us again."

"So what *are* you going to do? You going to see your parents?"

"Not until we've seen yours," he said firmly. "Not until we've cleared our names."

Kate snorted. "And just how do we do that?"

"I don't know. But until then we can't turn to anyone for help." He swallowed hard. "When I see my mom and dad again, I want them to see *me*, Tom Anderson, as I used to be."

"You think things can ever be the same after all we've been through?"

"Not the same," Tom said. "But maybe better. *Because* of what we've been through."

"We have to make it count for something, right?" She rolled her eyes, but Tom heard softness in her voice. "Give me a break. Stop being so damn good, saying the right things all the time."

"Okay." He smiled wryly. There was so much he wished he could say to her. "You look a total mess."

"Don't push it, Anderson!" He ducked as she threw her pillow at him. But when he looked at her again, he saw the worry in her eyes. "I wonder where they've gone now . . . *my* parents."

Tom sighed. "What we need is a psychic."

"Uh-huh." Kate suddenly seemed to brighten. "And I know where we can find a couple." Kate crossed to Stacy's PC. "See if we can get online. I haven't touched base with the geek community in days. Maybe someone's heard something about the lupines."

Tom smiled wryly. "Right. That paranormal chat room you hang out in?"

She nodded as she connected and signed in—as Troll Lover, her online alter ego.

"No way!" she cried, making Tom jump.

He looked over her shoulder. "What?"

"A message from Adam Blood," she said, her hands flying to her mouth in excitement. "Sent this morning."

"Genuine?" asked Tom nervously.

"Only two people in the world know I call myself Troll Lover. You and him."

"Well, what does he say?"

Quickly she typed in a password and hit the enter button.

Dear Trolly,

Hope you are as sexy as ever—and hope Tom isn't ripping his way through a new wardrobe every week (down, boy!). Heard a whisper—something big, secret, scary, and wolfy is going down in Chicago sometime soon. All the pureblood clans have been summoned by Takapa. . . . So in case you happen to be in Chicago right now—GET YOUR STUPID ARSES OUT OF THERE! And if not, AVOID LIKE THE BLOODY PLAGUE IF YOU HAVE ANY SENSE!

AB

"It sounds like him," said Tom dryly.

"Well?" Kate looked up at him. "Am I as sexy as ever? You know, with red hair?"

"He's such a kidder." Tom turned so she wouldn't see his blushes. "But I guess now we have a fair idea where Takapa's holed up. *And* your mom and dad."

"Better than a psychic," Kate said thoughtfully. "You meant what you said, didn't you? About needing to finish this . . ."

Tom nodded, took a deep breath, and turned to face her. "I hear Chicago's lovely this time of year."

"Then I guess," Kate replied, with the tiniest of smiles, "maybe we should check it out." She turned back to the computer and typed a brief reply:

> Dearest AB,
>   Too sexy for sense, too broke to keep running. We're going to Chicago. See you there?
>   XO, Troll Lover

"You never put kisses on notes to me!" Tom protested.

She sent the message and smiled innocently. "Don't I?"

Kate slept for most of the afternoon. Rest came easier now that she'd cleared things up with Tom. She knew he was right. He was facing up to the future, and she had to as well. Whatever it held.

A fresh change of clothes had been left out for her on the floor along with her backpack. She dressed quickly and went out to find Tom.

He was sitting in Rico's room, dressed more normally now in blue jeans that fit and a gray ribbed T-shirt. She watched him waiting in gloomy silence while the boy lay sleeping. It must be tough for Tom, she knew, with his parents just down the hall.

"Hey," he said softly, his face brightening as she walked over.

"Where'd you get the clothes?" she asked.

"Jasmine retrieved them from the hangout, along with our gear." Tom tapped his own backpack and sighed. "I think they were Ramon's. She didn't want them tossed out in the trash."

Kate nodded and turned to look at Rico. "He seems so peaceful."

"Just how peaceful this place will be when he wakes up remains to be seen," Tom said. "Have you noticed he's kind of a troublemaker?"

Kate smiled. "Where's Jasmine, anyway? I thought she'd be here."

"She's been busy."

Kate turned to see Stacy walking into the room with a welcoming smile.

"But she's going to be busier," Stacy added.

"She is?" Kate queried.

"Uh-huh. She's out front, waiting for you guys." Stacy held out her hand to Kate. "Goodbye. I'd say it's been a pleasure, but that wouldn't be strictly true."

Kate looked at Tom. "We're leaving already? How're we getting to Chicago?"

"I think it's going to work out," said Stacy, helping

Tom struggle into his backpack. "But I'm trying to steer clear of the details. I'm already an accessory to God knows how much. . . ."

Tom shook Stacy's hand. "Goodbye. Thanks for everything. Especially for looking after my parents."

"I'm going to have to spin them one hell of a line to explain why they've spent the last thirty-six hours in isolation," she said dryly, "but I'll make sure they know your last sighting was somewhere on the way to Hawaii."

He grinned. "You've done so much for us already."

Stacy shook her head. "Before you two came here, I was doing more harm than good." She smiled. "Now maybe I can turn that around. With some help from my friends."

Stacy crossed the room to check on Rico.

Kate fumbled in her purse for the picture Polar had snapped when she and Tom had first arrived at the tenement. Ramon stood between them, scowling in the middle of the picture: his old, habitual look. She placed the picture on Rico's bedside table. "Someone to watch over you," she whispered.

Then she and Tom left the room.

Jasmine was out in the parking lot, leaning against a glossy black Chrysler that seemed to shine in the wintry sunlight. "Thought you might need some wheels," she said. "Friend of Ramon's fixed up the plates. Should get you where you need to go without the cops on your tail."

Kate hoped Tom's dazed stare was due to the car and not the sight of Jasmine in her leather pants and fitted top.

"I don't know what to say," Tom said finally.

Jasmine snorted. "Then get out of here already."

"What are you going to do now?" Kate asked her.

"Not stealing no more cars, for one thing," she said. "Stacy's rule."

"Stacy?"

"She finally got her way. Fixed me up with a job, helping out with one of her hard luck programs." Jasmine shrugged. "Guess I ain't got much to go back to now. So I'm thinking I can help out the howler kids now the fighting's over . . . help them work stuff out."

"Kids like Polar?" Tom asked.

Jasmine glared at him. Then her face softened. "Maybe. I guess. Stacy says we have to give them for real what they thought they were getting from Takapa. Self-respect. You know?"

Tom nodded. "We know."

"Don't pay much. But Stacy knows a hostel where me and Rico can stay." She shrugged. "It's something."

"It's *really* something," Tom said. "And you are, too."

He went to kiss her cheek, but Jasmine pulled away. "Just take care of yourself, Tommy."

Tom opened the door of the Chrysler, threw his pack into the back, and climbed in the driver's seat.

Kate waited till he'd shut the door, then crossed to Jasmine. "I never thanked you for that stunt with the cigarettes," she said. "You saved my life."

"So I did." Jasmine eyed Kate. "Tom's in love with you, the poor bastard. You knew that, right?"

Kate took a step back involuntarily. "What did you say?"

"Guess it's just the way life works out." Jasmine shook her head. "Take care of him, 'kay?"

Kate nodded and crossed to the car's passenger side, doing her best not to show she was trembling.

Tom turned the ignition and backed the car out of the lot.

Kate saw Jasmine in the rearview, watching them go, hands on hips. Her figure dwindled, then vanished as Tom swung the car out into traffic.

"Penny for your thoughts," she murmured.

"I'm saving my pennies. We'll need them if we're going to eat tonight." He frowned. "Know any good diners on the way to Chicago?"

Kate smiled and fastened her seat belt, settling in for the long drive. "We'll find one," she said.